THE DIAMOND KID

When Deputy Marshal Dan Moore received a threatening letter intimating that his old enemy, Kid Diamond, was due for release, he had to leave town and seek out his enemies to safeguard the lives of innocent townsfolk. Accompanied by Barney Malone, a wandering artist, he went looking for the gang. His first clash with the Kid almost ended in his death, but he survived and fought back. The climax to the struggle came near an isolated house where Dan took on the gang, who had kidnapped a doctor's wife . . .

DAVID BINGLEY

---◆---

THE
DIAMOND KID

Complete and Unabridged

LINFORD
Leicester

First published in Great Britain in 1972

First Linford Edition
published 2005

British Library CIP Data

Bingley, David
    The Diamond Kid.—Large print ed.—
Linford western library
1. Western stories
2. Large type books
I. Title
823.9'14 [F]

    ISBN 1–84617–012–5

Published by
F. A. Thorpe (Publishing)
Anstey, Leicestershire

Set by Words & Graphics Ltd.
Anstey, Leicestershire
Printed and bound in Great Britain by
T. J. International Ltd., Padstow, Cornwall

This book is printed on acid-free paper

1

Dan Moore, the deputy town marshal of Conchas Creek, Santa Fe County, in the north of New Mexico territory, stiffened to alertness in the shadow afforded by the awning outside the peace office.

Daylight had almost gone. It was Saturday night, perhaps the busiest night of the week for a keeper of the peace, and someone had just created a loud noise in one of the outer thoroughfares. Dan listened and a stream of similar noises followed in quick succession. He relaxed a little, realizing that he was hearing some sort of a fire cracker, rather than the blasts of a revolver.

His right hand came away from the holster at his hip. He breathed deeply and stuck his thumb in the belt at his waist. The four saloons were busy. They would sell more beer and whiskey than in the two previous nights put together. And, consequently, there would be more drunks. More citizens slightly out of control. Some would need help. Others a little persuasion, and possibly one or two would lose control, fire off their weapons or embark upon a fight which might end in a wounding or a death.

Unless Dan could get there in time to prevent the worst. Jabex Marshman, the town marshal, was out of town on a visit to his kin. The other deputy, a Mexican, was down with a fever. That left only Dan, himself, and old Limpy Rogers, who doubled as jailer and general handyman around the office. And Marshal Marshman believed in letting the townsmen wear their guns on all occasions.

Dan yawned. He thought that Jabez, at fifty-six, was a little past his best, and that he was trying to run the town by being on the best of terms with everybody. Dan knew, and maybe Jabez, too, that someone, some time, would challenge their authority, and then it would be a matter of answering the challenge with quick gun play. Dan felt that there were few determined gunmen that Jabez was fast enough to beat to the draw, and that could lead to a truly serious situation. It was time for Jabez to think about retiring. But he never mentioned such a matter.

Dan thought about rolling a cigarette, but peals of laughter from down the street made him think otherwise. He began a slow walk down the sidewalk, his eyes and ears very much on the alert. As he walked, he massaged an old bullet scar above his right hip. He had acquired that in his days as a deputy to the county sheriff when hunting outlaws.

The groove had healed, but before it had done so it had affected his riding. He had tried to occupy his saddle with his body slightly out of balance so as not to aggravate the wound, and, consequently, during a fast mounted chase, he had lost balance and made a fall which had jarred his hip.

The hip injury had put him out of action for a while. A doctor had recommended that he took a job where less riding was necessary. Pains in the hip had made him take the advice and so he had stopped being a sheriff's deputy and instead taken up this appointment, policing a town. In a town far removed from his earlier exploits.

Horse riding had become a very infrequent form of exercise for him, and there were times when he wondered if he would ever be as good on the back of a horse again. He had his doubts, although he kept them to himself.

Music drifted up an intersection, played on an old upright honkie-tonk piano, and backed by two guitars. A Mexican with a rather husky voice sang a plaintive melody which appeared to be pleasing the drinkers whose first language was Spanish. Further along Main Street, two more saloons vied with each other over the trade. Jenny's Place and the Broken Horseshoe. Dan knew which he preferred. He was more than a little attracted to Jennifer Braid, the owner of Jenny's Place, while the owner of the Broken Horseshoe, Zeke Starr, boasted that he had earned his money by gambling and certain illegal practices before he started up as a saloon owner.

Dan ignored the raucous male-voice songs which were coming out of the Broken Horseshoe. Instead, he moved towards the batwings of the saloon owned by the woman. He stepped through the doors, pushing aside one half with each shoulder. Once inside, he lowered his eyes to adjust to the change of light, standing quite still for almost half a minute.

The big room was a hive of noise. The shouting of men, the stamping of feet; the clink of glasses and the creaking of chairs. Swirling smoke from countless cigarettes, cigars and tobacco pipes climbed towards the ceiling, drifting slowly around the bowls of the hanging lamps.

His speedy, silent entry drew many eyes. Some just glanced at the star pinned to the left pocket of his check shirt. Others showed more curiosity, weighing him up as a keeper of the peace.

Dan stood a little under six feet tall, a sinewy young man in his late twenties with dark healthy hair, which he parted at the left side and wore long in sideburns. His lean, sunburned face was on the narrow side, cleanshaven and in no way remarkable, except for the intense green eyes which often gave people the impression that he was staring when such was not the case.

His stetson was fairly new, being made of good quality black material and worn flat at the crown. He made an imposing figure, with his feet planted slightly apart in well polished black riding boots.

Two or three men who knew him called to him by name.

'Evening, Dan! How's the town behaving itself?'

'Evenin' deputy. Anybody keepin' you company yet, in the cells?'

He nodded and smiled to several people, but made no attempt to answer any of the half-humorous sallies. All the time they were greeting him he was weighing up the general situation. If anything, the saloon was more packed than it had been on the two previous Saturdays. Jenny would be pleased, just so long as the crowds did not get out of hand, and that was one way in which he could help her.

His questing eyes sought her out, but she remained hidden from him for a time. His attention was taken by a dense crowd of people at the opposite side to the card tables. The stove in that direction was not lit and the piano was elsewhere. For a time, he wondered what it was that attracted so many people.

He pushed his way in that direction and what he saw surprised him. In a tiny cleared space, a stranger, a young man with longish wavy hair the colour of ripe corn was drawing the likeness of one of the town characters, 'Parson' James Rowell. Rowell's face, lit up with many whiskies and carelessly shaven, made him look all of his fifty-five years. He was wearing, as always, a battered Quaker-style hat with a broad brim and a soiled necktie under a winged collar.

Dan's alert eyes took in the deft way in which the artist worked. The pencil in the moving hand seemed almost magical, as Parson's head and shoulders appeared upon a piece of paper some two feet square in the minimum number of lines. Detail followed detail, even the veins in the whites of his eyes being depicted.

A wag called out: 'Hey, Parson, you'll have to behave yourself after this, otherwise the marshal will use your picture for a reward notice!'

Loud guffaws of laughter followed this comment. Dan grinned broadly and nodded to the elusive saloon owner, who was sitting to one side in a low-cut, off-the-shoulder bottle green evening gown. Jennifer was quite a beauty with her violet eyes, faint freckles and finely-chiselled features. And hers had been the first pencil portrait attempted that night by the artist.

Her picture was propped up beside her on a makeshift easel made out of a hat rack. Dan looked from the smiling young woman to the picture and back again. The long brown hair, rich in highlights, had been carefully copied. Likewise the centre parting and the ringlets which dangled easily over small white ears. And there was a suggestion of her shapeliness lower down.

'How do you like my work, deputy?' the artist asked.

The observers round about went quiet, anticipating his reply. Jenny licked her lips unconsciously, while Parson began to shoot uncertain glances in his direction. Dan blinked, for once embarrassed. He hesitated and

9

when the violet eyes of the owner looked troubled, he thought hard.

'Well, I'd say the likenesses were very good. Yes, definitely good. However I still prefer the sitter rather than the picture, at least, in one case.'

The listeners gave out with a low murmur of applause, which swelled appreciably as the full purport of his words was understood. Jenny blushed rather prettily. Her agile mind came to her aid.

'There now, Parson. You heard what Dan said? He'd rather have you than your portrait! Ain't that a compliment? Ain't it jest?'

More laughter, and more stamping of the feet. Parson lost his composure and shifted his pose. The artist straightened up, good-naturedly, and grinned in Dan's direction. Perhaps another score of curious drinkers were moving towards the artist and his work.

Dan quickly sized up the situation and decided it was time for him to move out again. He liked chatting with

Jenny, but she was more or less inaccessible now. He would return later.

'I've got some more walkin' to do,' he called across to her.

She nodded and gave him an expression which suggested that she fully understood. He pushed his way in the general direction of the exit. Just before he stepped out into the open air, he glanced back. The owner had risen to her feet. She was standing behind the young artist who had resumed his work. Something about the absorbed way in which she watched him needled the young peace officer. He wondered with interest if what he was feeling could be termed jealousy.

Somehow, jealousy seemed to him to be an unmanly emotion. He shrugged away the feeling as the fresh night air fanned his face. His steps were quicker as he continued with his rounds. Nothing worthy of note occurred until he was approaching the fourth of the town's saloons.

The Bonanza lacked paint and style,

but somehow its owner contrived to get a small clientele into the building. It was obvious from quite a distance that a hard core of seasoned drinkers were still busy in the place. Raucous male voices were singing unmusically an old gold-miners' song, accompanied by a mouth harp. The singing was still in full swing when two figures came staggering through the swinging doors. The first man was a shaggy forty-year old in soiled trail clothes. He made his exit under his own power, flicking upwards from time to time at a broken hat brim which annoyed him.

His drinking partner was older; a rheumy-eyed fellow in a battered derby hat. His buttonless top coat failed to conceal the double-breasted waistcoat over his promising paunch. He came out with the benefit of the owner's propelling boot, and he was in a filthy temper.

For a few moments, the two men did not notice the deputy making his way along the boards. The older man, who answered to Zack, made a grab for his holster, but missed it on account of his clothing getting in the way.

'I want to go back in there, Randy! You know me, I can't stand these superior saloon owners showin' me the street. Let's get in there an' decorate his walls with a few lead slugs!'

Randy saw the star on Dan's shirt. At once he shushed his partner and did his best to straighten him up.

'No, Zack, not now. The owner was kind of upset by us in there. He wouldn't like it if we disfigured his walls. Neither would this deputy who's comin' along here right now, especially to talk to us. You see how it is? You an' me, we ought to be findin' our way to that roomin' house. It ain't good business to hire a room an' then not use the bed. So let's go, huh?'

Dan stepped abruptly down into the dirt. By that time, the older man, Zack, was taking more than a passing interest in him. Randy sought to turn him round and head him up the street, but

Zack was not yet ready to conform.

'Evenin', deputy,' Zack remarked, 'it sure is a quiet night for the end of the week. How's about steppin' in to the Bonanza with us for a last drink? What do you say to that for a suggestion?'

'I'd say if anyone was to press me that you had had enough already, amigo. As for me, I have my job to do, an' I can't hang about right now. So how about makin' your way to your bed, an' sleepin' this one off?'

Dan paused beside the pair and looked them over closely. It was clear that Randy had much better control of himself than Zack.

'Think you can get him to your room without help?'

Randy nodded. 'Sure enough, deputy, he'll be okay. He jest likes to run off at the mouth when he's had a few drinks. Don't make anything out of it. He'll go quiet when you've moved on.'

Dan thought that Randy was probably right. He nodded, stroked his chin, and moved on, staying in the middle of the street. He had only gone a yard or so when Zack started to mutter.

'He don't have the right to tell a citizen of the United States he's had enough to drink! He's actin' big behind that badge! I've a good mind to . . . '

The voice tailed off as Randy saw danger and wrestled with Zack. The older man had pulled his gun and was seeking to aim it in Dan's direction. His intention, no doubt, was to fire an odd bullet fairly close to the deputy's feet, but the drink played havoc with his aim, and before Randy could stop him the revolver was discharged. A bullet flew just wide of Dan's knee. In a flash, the deputy turned and drew his own weapon, questing urgently for a target.

At the same time, Randy had thrown himself upon Zack, only to be brushed aside. As soon as Randy saw Dan crouching and ready to fire he stepped well to one side and threw up his hands. Zack continued to weave, waving his gunhand and the weapon in it. He kept blinking his eyes as though he could not see straight.

'Zack, will you stop wavin' that gun, for Pete's sake?'

Randy sounded more than a little scared of the outcome. Dan, himself, was rather shaken. A bullet through the knee could have crippled him for life. He felt that he should have been alert to this sneak attack, and that his own reaction gun-wise ought to have been a lot quicker and more effective.

He was breathing deeply as he bore down upon the drunken gunman. There was a second or two of extreme tension before he got within snatching distance of the gun, but he succeeded in what he set out to do. As soon as Zack was disarmed, Randy laid a friendly hand on Dan's shoulder. He stepped back as it was brushed off.

'Do — do you have to lock him up, deputy?'

'After an attempt upon my life? I certainly do. He's a menace an' you know it. Now, get out of my way.'

'I'll help you take him along,' Randy

offered, his breath reeking of beer.

'One drunk at a time is all I need, brother. Keep away from me. If you must help, get along to the peace office an' tell the old man in there that our first customer is on his way.'

Randy acted upon the advice. For a time, he had difficulty in keeping up with the deputy's rate of progress. But the weight of Zack's body soon began to tire Dan. Although the drunk had the use of his legs, he did not help much. Gradually the man with the broken hat brim drew ahead.

Dan began to wonder if the evening was going to deteriorate as far as keeping the peace was concerned.

2

As usual on a Saturday night, Limpy
Rogers, the town jailer, was in a gay,
devil-may-care mood. His long wisps of
white moustache were as limp as ever,
but his watery eyes twinkled and the
gap-toothed grin with which he wel-
comed Dan and the drunk might have
been put to better use in the foyer of a
prosperous hotel.

'Welcome back, Dan, my boy. I see
you have a prisoner. His friend was
kind enough to come along in advance
an' tell me we had a guest. Tell me, is
he likely to be one of those we put in
the front cell where we can see him all
the time, or would you say he's the type
for the back corridor? Me, I'd say he
was a sturdy hombre who had seen
better days.'

Dan kicked the door closed behind
him and casually slipped Zack into an

upright chair. Randy, Zack's friend, hovered about in the background and that made the winded deputy even more cross than before.

'Doggone it, mister, are you still hangin' about here? Get out before I find you draughty lodgings! Do you hear me?'

Dan glowered at the unwanted visitor and took half a pace towards him. That was sufficient to have Randy headed for the door at the run. He touched his broken hat brim once and then disappeared from view. Apart from Dan's laboured breathing, the office was alive with Limpy's high-pitched cackle.

Limpy remarked: 'I can tell by the expression on your face this hombre is goin' down the corridor. Did he do anything special, before you brought him in?'

'Only tried to blow a hole through my knee, from behind,' Dan grumbled bitterly. 'Go ahead of me. Open up the corridor and the far cell, an' hurry it up. After that, I want you to go out an' get your supper 'cause this town is still very much alive an' I want to be free to do some more patrollin'. Think you can eat quickly, for once?'

Limpy killed a jest before it was uttered. He blew his cheeks, sending his long strands of moustache sideways. He shrugged and moved to do Dan's bidding. When he moved fast, as he was doing now, it was clear that one of his legs was shorter than the other.

Zack straightened out on the upright chair. The wall connected with his hat brim. He snored for a second or so, and then roused himself. Before he could sort out his surroundings, Dan grabbed an arm and hung it round his shoulder, hauling the bulky fellow to his feet.

Three minutes later, the drunk was in the rearmost cell, hastily tugging a coarse blanket around his cool frame on the wooden bench provided. Limpy, who had a good appetite, hurried away to get his food without further comment.

Dan rolled himself a smoke in the cell corridor, and for a minute or two, he allowed his troubled gaze to dwell upon the blanketed figure.

He was thinking about the sneak gun shot which might so easily have disabled him. There had been a time when his senses had been so keen that he would have sensed the danger in time to duck, turn about and retaliate satisfactorily. A man with a badge such as he wore, and one who had enemies, such as he had, could not afford to be slow on the draw.

Zack snored loudly and on a varying note. The insistent sound broke in upon Dan's thoughts and drove him back to the office. He was careful about the way he locked the cell door and the one which gave access to the corridor. He had once worked for an officer who lost a prisoner through carelessness with keys.

He sat himself down upon the scarred surface of the marshal's desk and put his boots on the chair.

A slow draw, and enemies. It was over two years since he had been instrumental in the capture of the notorious Kid Diamond, who had — as a consequence — gone to the territorial penitentiary. The Kid had gone to do his stint for armed robbery and a killing swearing eternal vengeance against Dan Moore, and there was something in the way he said his piece in court which made even the judge believe that he would remember his hate until he was freed.

The Kid had been caught unawares, when he thought his rear was covered by one of his gang. Some of his underlings had also been caught but three of the more notorious had split up and stayed free, ever since, so far as Dan was aware. There had been rumours of robberies from time to time in Many Springs County where all the hunting had gone on, but no one in that widespread area, which was to the south of Santa Fe County, could really have said for sure that the crimes had been committed by members of the Kid's old gang.

Dan found himself shaking his head over the situation, although there was no one around to see him. For a time, he forgot about the town and his duty to police it. He was seeing in his mind's eye the images of the outlaws he had once hunted.

The Kid himself was a handsome fellow in his middle thirties with full sensuous lips and eyes like bullet tips. At some stage in his career his left upper eyelid had been split. It had not healed properly, so that when he blinked slowly it tended to give strangers the jitters. Most of the time when he was gang leading, he sported a straw hat with a snakeskin band. His ample hair was of a brown shade and he sometimes grew a thin moustache. His height, his manner and his power of command made him the natural leader.

Prominent among his followers was Nevada Tom. Tom was a few years older than the Kid. He was as tall, but thinner. He had a broad flat face. His dead pan eyes did not have the advantage of brows. His crisp black hair was well matched with the black trail clothes which he wore habitually.

Bruce McGillie was broad-faced with a fair spade beard. His eyes, which could strike fear without effort, were a pale shade of blue. His hair had receded at the forehead. As a consequence, he wore his round black hat almost always.

The Corsican, as Pierre Ludeau was called, happened to be the youngest by a year. He was short, thick-chested and broad in the trunk. He exuded menace in an entirely different way from the others. Perhaps it had something to do with his bulbous eyes, his over-long arms and his very short dark hair which had a sprinkling of grey highlights in it.

Kid Diamond, Nevada Tom, Bruce McGillie and the Corsican. What a combination, Dan was thinking. They would take a lot of stopping if they ever got together again, and it was possible that they might unite, if the others were around when the Kid got his discharge.

He was trying to reckon up how much longer his old enemy had to do in time before his discharge when Limpy came breezing back into the building, burping over his supper.

★　★　★

The time was not far short of midnight. Usually, the sounds of merrymaking had faded by that hour. Those in business who still had clients, other than gamblers, had then to make up their minds whether to further encourage their clients, or to persuade them to leave.

Jennifer Braid had a sharp eye for business. She had the happy knack of making men feel warm inside. With a small gesture, a smile or little more, she could make them think that they had a special place in her thoughts, though if the truth were known she cared little for them.

On this particular evening, the visiting artist had done a lot to boost her trade. She admitted that to herself. His likeness of her had pleased her. She wondered how best she could use it. Should it be kept to drum up business, in a public room? Or should she keep it in her private apartment? She supposed that other young women in a better position than herself would present it to an admirer, and hope that he would propose.

As she circulated, on the quiet side of the big smoke-laden room, she shrugged rather prettily in the revealing bottle green gown, and considered her prospects. No one at all, rich or poor, attracted her in the whole of the town, other than Dan Moore, the deputy. And Dan brooded a lot, took his job very seriously. Her saloon kept her tied down for long hours most days of the week. Although there was something more than ordinary friendship between Dan and her, their relationship seemed to lack the impetus to develop into anything more significant.

She found herself pouting without quite knowing why when another outburst of laughter went up from the group still surrounding the artist. His crumpled Texas-rolled hat was even further back on his head now. It appeared almost to be resting on his ears. He had consumed a fair quantity of beer, and yet his drawing hand was still busy, and still as cunning as ever.

Jenny felt herself drawn towards the young man. Was it a simple case of the attraction of a man for a woman, or was he tapping her maternal feelings? There was something appealing about the fellow. It was as if he needed to have his work approved by all who saw it. Jenny wondered whether she should go across and join the group. She felt tired because of the hour. A slight feeling of lethargy made her decide against a further show of gaiety on her part. Besides, Dan had hinted that he would be back. He could appear at any time.

For the first time, she had the image

of the deputy alongside that of the fair-headed newcomer. They contrasted interestingly, but because of her general tiredness, she did not attempt to compare them at all. Scarcely masking a yawn, she walked soundlessly across the rear of the room towards her office. Once there, she kicked off her shoes and raised her feet on a cushion.

★ ★ ★

The artist started to be known when he scribbled his signature at the base of his drawings. For those who could not readily decipher the scribble, he admitted to being one Barney Malone of no fixed address.

Around the time when Jenny briefly retired it was clear that there were no other clients prepared to pay for their likenesses to be drawn, and, consequently, Barney continued to draw to entertain those around him. He drew because of his inner compulsion to draw and because the beer had put him in a particularly good mood.

Two large sheets of paper had been discarded to no particular purpose, and now he was drawing the rough outline of a man's hat and face without knowing quite what to put in it. From time to time, he straightened his back, and briefly surveyed the features on show around him.

He had the benefit of a close ring and beyond that, a looser circle of those still more interested in liquor than the wiles of his pencil. Many of the faces interested him, but one in particular drew his gaze more than the others.

Those who were closest, seeing that he was trying to make up his mind about something, encroached still further, making guesses as to whose features they would soon recognize. Men argued, and the arguments promoted greater interest. Barney listened to them and he held back on the more revealing details as long as he could.

Eventually, however, he had to make the pencil strokes which began to finalize the portrait. Speculation grew again. Men regarded each other and shook their heads. Some kept reasonably quiet, hoping that something of their own make-up would appear and that they would be the centre of attraction for a while.

In a very short time it became clear that Barney's last subject was not one of those who were showing most interest in his work. Feeling slightly off-put the admirers turned their heads and looked elsewhere. Men on the fringe of the group had their interest enlivened and still the identity of the subject was not clear.

One disgruntled character remarked: 'Doggone it, the kid's havin' us on. There ain't nobody in the buildin' with a face like that!'

Some frowned. Others turned to their drink, slightly discouraged. Barney took a deep breath and hastily brought his work to a finish. In little more than a minute he added a squarish, ragged, dark beard and a pair of eyes which should have been significant anywhere.

The eyes were set in marked hollows, rather too close together and ill-matched. One eye appeared to be more prominent than the other and it was out of alignment. Abruptly, the inner circle of observers broke up. They roved the full length and breadth of the room, staring in others' faces, searching out the man with the beard.

At last they found him. He was seated alone at the long bar, sipping tepid beer and seeking the company of nobody. Barney had seen his homely face reflected in the long mirror. It was in that mirror that this fellow first noticed that he was the centre of attraction.

Men came up on either side and stared at him. Some grimaced, others laughed, but all were impressed. The bearded one tensed up and grew angry. He slid off his stool and pushed back his leather half coat, probing for his gun belt.

'Now see here,' he began, 'I came in

jest to drink an' I ain't interferin' with no one. So back off, all of you, unless you're trouble bent.'

A man whose laugh was a little off-key sought to put things right. He pointed away in the direction of the stove and the artist.

'Shucks, amigo, nobody ain't seekin' to infringe upon your private thoughts, but that there young hombre over there, the artist, has jest drawn your face so that you could pick yourself out of a thousand. Go over an' take a look at it, why don't you?'

The bearded man seemed slow to take in what had been said, but his attitude to those immediately around him changed. He let out a noise which some would describe as a snarl, and hastened over towards the stove and the young man who was dusting the sweatband of his side-rolled hat.

On the way over, he barged one man who was too drunk to care and separated two others who were still sober enough to be resentful. His impetus took him into the front ring of observers and there he saw the likeness of himself on paper for the first time. He frowned and stepped back half a pace, his red underlip moving as though out of control.

Deep emotions welled up inside him. He turned upon the artist who was pushing one of his pencil stubs into his breast pocket and pointed a grubby forefinger at him. He was not a man of words, but anger helped on this occasion.

'Now see here, young fellow, bein' an artist don't give you the right to draw jest anyone you please. I ain't seekin' publicity an' I object to everyone pointin' their finger at me. I got a right not to be noticed if I want it that way.'

The angry man turned his attention to the board on which his likeness was pinned. He made a grab at it, and Barney, who had thought of trying to mollify him, changed his mind and sought to prevent his interfering with the portrait. Consequently, they collided. The board went over with a loud bang, and those who could sense a fight backed off a little way.

In a matter of seconds, Barney Malone and his new enemy were throwing haymaking punches at one another. Barney took two in the face which freshened his already fresh complexion and put a glint in his blue eyes which ordinarily looked to be too relaxed.

He scored to the chest and managed to land one on the side of his opponent's head, but the bearded man was heavily built and not yet out of breath. The latter's boring tactics paid off in a couple of rushes. Observers gave more ground, taking chairs with them, and as often happens in a crowd who have drunk a lot, their sympathies in many cases began to change.

Barney was perhaps just beginning to get the better of the exchanges when someone from a distance hurled an empty bottle. It crashed against his hatless head with stunning force and dropped him to the floor.

At the same time, Dan Moore erupted into the middle and grabbed the upright fighter as he prepared to work out his anger with the use of his booted feet. The bearded man struggled and his ill assorted eyes suggested that there was a lot more fight in him.

Dan's badge was dislodged in the struggle, and when it fell to the floor, significantly, it brought about a change in the struggling man. Dan was pushed back, and he stayed that way, straddling the unconscious body of Barney. The other appeared to calm down. He backed off, worked his way through the silent watchers and headed through the batwings without a backward glance.

3

Normally, Dan might have sought to delay the departure of one of the battlers, but he knew that Jenny was not in favour of incurring the law and that she did not like her clients to be mixed up with peace officers.

The deputy stood with his hands on his hips, taking in the faces of all those who still seemed interested in the goings on. They were abnormally silent now, and somewhat cowed in the face of Dan's probing looks. While they waited for him to say something about the near brawl, Jenny pushed her way through them and came to a halt at the front of the gathering.

Her finger tips went to her mouth as she glanced down at the body of the fallen man. While she was looking, Barney began to stir. At the same time he groaned and his right hand started to explore the back of his head.

Dan's shaded eyes sought out the owner, trying to read something into her expression. All she showed was anxiety. She had no reason to try and make Dan act in any particular way.

'I'd like personally to lay my hands on the gentle soul who threw that bottle,' Dan remarked calmly. 'So, if the gent in question is still with us, now is the time for him to explain.'

He talked like a man cold sober, which was about right, and his words brought his listeners out of the warm mental haze engendered by their drinking. They shifted their feet somewhat uneasily and started to glance at one another as though no one was quite clear as to who had thrown the bottle. Dan had noted the general direction from which the missile had come, but that was all. The watchers had been shifting about, moving this way and that, so as not to miss a punch. He did not think that anyone was likely to tell him what he wanted to know.

Barney Malone stirred beneath him. Dan shifted his feet out of the fallen man's way, but his eyes were soon back upon the drinkers.

'All right, then, if you choose to keep it a secret. The next best thing is to crawl off to your homes. I'm not at all sure I'd want a pack like you for my friends. You didn't have to wait long to turn against the artist, here. He had many enemies when I arrived besides the bottle thrower.

'So why don't you clear out? Get to your beds. There'll be more time to drink another day. You've had your-selves a lot of fun, an' Miss Jenny, here, is tired. One look at her face is enough to tell you that.'

Dan glanced sharply into a few of the more obvious faces. He then turned his attention to Barney, helping him to stretch out on a long bench and examining the contusion on the back of his head. Already it had raised a promising lump.

Jenny came across to him and laid a

gentle hand on his arm.

'I'm glad you were there when things got a little out of hand, Dan. I was out back, restin' my legs an' I must have dozed off in the chair. The next thing I knew, there was this uproar. Is his head badly damaged?'

By this time, Barney had raised himself on one elbow. He grinned rather sheepishly at the two people bending over him. 'Thanks for your help, deputy. I suppose the other fellow has gone now, huh?'

'Yer, he's gone, all right.' Dan glanced behind him and saw that most of the roisterers had already left the building. 'That likeness you did of the bearded man, it must have been uncomplimentary for him to attack you like that.'

Barney glanced in the direction of the fallen board. The picture was on the underside, and nobody made a move to turn it over. He shook his head rather sadly.

'I think it was a good one,' he said

calmly. 'I'd drunk a lot of beer but I took some pains about it. Maybe it was too *good* for him. In any case, that's an interestin' consideration. By the way, what are you proposin' to do with me? Do I get locked up for breakin' the peace?'

Dan shrugged. He did not answer right away. Instead, he waited for Jenny to return from the bar with a glass of whiskey. She had heard what Barney said, and she knew they had to talk this thing out.

'Do you think that bearded jasper will come after you again?' Dan queried thoughtfully.

'I shouldn't think it's likely,' Barney commented. 'He was probably riled because all the others were bawling at him. Don't use him as an excuse to put me away for my own safety.'

He stopped stroking back his tousled hair and shot Jenny an enquiring glance.

'Does he have to be locked up, Dan?' she asked, a plea in her voice.

'It'd be safest. Nobody could easily get at him in my office.' Dan turned to further scrutinise the artist. 'Where would you sleep if I left you to look after yourself?'

The fair man grinned, showing good teeth. Before he could answer, however, Jenny spoke up. 'I've given him the use of the shed at the back. Nobody knows he's moved his gear in there. I guess he'll be safe for the rest of the night. Is that where you'd like to be, Barney?'

The tired owner sounded terribly anxious that everything should suit the young artist in every way. Dan noted this, and wondered why she was so solicitous of his welfare. He kept his private thoughts strictly to himself and wearily wondered if he had dealt with the last incident of the night. Barney was very keen to use the shed . . .

A tired barman with a sweeping brush waited for them to move out of the way and that was sufficient to kill Dan's concern about the artist and his immediate future. He explained what

41

he was going to do, and went off to the peace office for a last consultation with his lively old jailer.

*   *   *

Dan had a private arrangement with Jenny. At all times when the hotel part of the building was not packed to capacity he had the use of a room on the upper floor at the back. On this particular night he had been asleep for perhaps two hours when the strong smell of wood smoke drifted in through his window.

Tired as he was, he roused himself quite rapidly and crossed to the window. By standing on a chair he had a useful view of the rear of the hotel directly below him. Swirling smoke and flame coming from the shed which stood a few feet away from the rear wall, reminded him with a shock that the small wooden building was the temporary resting place of the fellow who answered to Barney Malone.

Somewhere down below, a person or persons started to cough. Dan found himself doing the same. He pulled back from his window, which was open near the top, and hastily grabbed for his clothing and boots. Here was a situation which called for immediate action and for much thought. Malone was in great danger, and as a secondary consideration the rear wall of the hotel, constructed entirely of wooden planking, might very well catch fire if something was not done about the danger quite quickly.

Dan clambered on the chair and stuck out his head. 'Hey, you down there! Malone, are you all right? If you can hear me, keep well away from the shed! Give the alarm!'

He withdrew his head, still fumbling with his pants, and knowing that Malone, if he had escaped, would not know how to give the alarm. Fortunately, there were sounds which indicated that others had been roused. As soon as he was properly dressed, Dan flung out of

43

the room. On the way downstairs he found time to reflect that Malone appeared to have the habit of attracting trouble.

★　★　★

Malone had been sleeping heavily on the narrow bench which was part of the hut's usual fittings when the fire started. He found out afterwards that someone had inserted quite a useful quantity of wood shavings through the open door and then casually put a match to them.

The slight breeze which came in through the door opening had been all that was necessary to start the conflagration. He had pushed the blanket off him, found the heat still oppressive and then awakened. His senses had cleared almost at once. He retreated before the blaze and then found that he could go no further.

He had walls at his back, and the only other way out was through a small

44

window with glass in it. Necessity made him punch out the glass without hesitation. He stood on the bench with the backs of his legs suffering from the heat. In a way, it was fortunate that he had not bothered to undress. He tossed his boots through the opening, set his mouth in a hard line, and followed the boots, head first.

Luckily he had a drop of a few feet and that made it possible for him to do a partial somersault in the air and land on the back of his shoulders. He lay there for about half a minute, partially winded and seeing the burning shed with an awed look on his face from a peculiar angle.

For the first time, he thought about why the fire had occurred. He was certain that it had been done deliberately, but surely a man with a homely face would not go to such lengths to be rid of him? *Had* it been the man he had fought with, or did he have other enemies about whom he had no knowledge? A bottle thrower, for instance. Perhaps he was making up villains out of his imagination.

Through the smoke above the shed, he could see faces at the windows of the rear rooms. Shocked occupiers withdrew and closed the windows, no doubt hoping that in doing so they would deny the flames which flickered up towards them. One or two men appeared around the end of the building, but they retreated rather quickly until they could find some protection for their faces.

Suddenly a most disturbing thought shattered the young artist. All his drawings, the ones he carried about with him, were in that burning shack. He had no permanent home, but those drawings were of value to him. He rose to his knees, and then to his feet, his mind turning over the possibility of making a bid to rescue the sketches.

Some little distance away a bell was ringing, or some object which gave out a sound like a bell. That meant help would be forthcoming. But it would not come in time to save the shack, or any of its contents. In desperation, Barney tied his bandanna across his face and darted around to the side nearest the hotel, the one where the shed door was situated. His hastily donned boots were wrinkled on his calves.

A pall of black smoke drove him back at once. He tried again and managed to stamp on some of the rubble which had been put into the entrance to start the fire. A firefighter, all face-mask and protecting hat, came out of the smoke and hurled a bucket of water in through the door.

Barney, who had stepped back, had to throw himself on the ground to avoid being engulfed by smoke of a greater density. For nearly a minute, he coughed with his cheek against the earth. The contusion on the back of his head throbbed. He backed away, and some glimmering in his memory directed him to an old wooden water trough at the rear of the plot.

He was thinking of splashing himself

from head to foot when Dan Moore showed up at the other end.

'You all right?' Dan called harshly. Barney nodded. 'Give me a hand to move the trough!' the deputy went on.

Barney hesitated for a few seconds before complying. As they staggered forward, he tried to explain that he wanted to get back into the shed, but the raging flames drowned his voice, and when they managed to round the hut Dan had another use for the slopping water.

'Help me to raise it three feet in the air,' he thundered. 'Then take your timin' from me! Understand?'

Barney nodded. They managed the difficult manoeuvre, and when the trough was in the best position it was tilted in the direction of the hotel. Dan's idea had been to douse the wall, so that it would not catch fire from the burning shed.

Barney accepted Dan's plans, and for a time, they worked with teams of men who came down the alleys on either side of Jenny's building, forming lines and passing buckets. Initially, all the water was hurled at the burning hut.

In a relatively short time it had consumed itself, and more water was then aimed at the main building's rear. Dan withdrew before the fire-fighting was at an end. That sort of endeavour was not strictly his responsibility.

He took Barney in through the front of the saloon, had a brief chat with Jenny, who had been seriously worried by the latest development, and intimated that he was withdrawing to his office for the rest of the night.

He concluded: 'And Barney comes with me. For his own sake, an' his safety.'

Neither Jenny nor Barney appeared to be pleased by this pronouncement but they both knew when not to argue.

4

Around nine o'clock the following morning, a person unfamiliar to Barney Malone began to make himself at home in the big dusty office of the town marshal. In the cell which faced into the office, the singed and bruised artist came back to reality with some reluctance, and cocked an eye at the man who appeared to be so restless at that comparatively early hour.

According to Barney's basic thinking it ought to have been Dan Moore, the deputy, or the old limping fellow who acted as jailer. But the man who was opening the office window, and generally tidying up was neither of these, nor could he be envisaged as the town marshal, who had business elsewhere.

As Barney came up on one elbow, the visitor paused in his small, self-imposed tasks and courteously nodded to him, bowing from the waist and doffing his hat which was of a type not often seen in an ordinary cow town.

The prisoner murmured a gravelly greeting and tried to blink himself awake. He fingered the swelling on his head and came to the conclusion that it had ceased to grow, which provided consolation of a sort.

'You had quite a day, yesterday, young fellow, if you don't mind my saying so.'

Barney did not mind, but he was slow to make that clear. He was thinking that the visitor's speech was a little more refined than that of an ordinary citizen accustomed to Western ways. He used his eyes and learned a lot through doing so.

'I'm Victor Pardoe, formerly a doctor in this town, but now retired. I realize that it is a trifle inconsiderate of me to call at such an hour when you haven't had the chance to wash or to take breakfast, but I trust that my presence won't upset you in any way?'

51

As an answer seemed to be expected, Barney replied with an uncompromising nod. His eyes were still busy. Pardoe's hat was a neat narrow-brimmed one fashioned out of expensive black material almost as fine as silk. The top of it was flat. It had a black ribbon for a band.

Other items of the visitor's aspect were of interest, too. He was tall, and built on generous lines, inclining towards obesity. His magnificent chest had, at the age of fifty or a little more, blended in with a small but promising paunch, which a good tailor has masked well. A grey buttoned vest topped trousers of the same colour under a becoming cutaway coat of a darker shade. A red tie, held in place with a gold stick pin, gave Pardoe an air of distinction.

His hair was iron grey, as were his short jutting brows. A full, but unwrinkled face was cleanshaven. His eyes were alert and brown over a short broad nose which might have been forcibly spread a little in his youth.

Pardoe approached the bars of the cell, producing from his breast pocket a container of cigars. He pushed one through the bars and extracted another for himself. A single match did the job of lighting up both. Barney had a slight feeling of unreality, but he was prepared to go along with it for a while.

Pardoe returned to the marshal's desk. 'I've always been attracted to anyone who could capture the likeness of another, either in pencil or in paint. Perhaps you won't be offended if I do something to help foster your talent. I'm sure you won't object after that dreadful fire of last night.'

Barney was baffled and his expression showed it. He waited, and Pardoe picked up from the desk certain articles which he had brought along with him. There was a roll of white paper of a good quality, and a bundle of pencils held together with a piece of string. These, the visitor took along to the cell and offered to its occupant, along with a wooden board which could be used to rest the paper on.

The young man came to his feet and showed frank gratitude. Getting the right sort of paper and pencils was always difficult for him in his wanderings. He took the proffered gifts and sank back upon his wooden bench, seeing his benefactor in a new light.

Pardoe retired and waited for him to ask questions.

'How come you're in here at the same time as a prisoner, Mr Pardoe, when there's no peace officer about?'

The ex-doctor smiled indulgently and sank into the swivel chair which creaked under his weight. 'Oh, it's nothing, really. I'm well known in these parts, you see. Dan Moore stirred himself early. He wanted to get his breakfast and make an early tour of the town, so I said I'd stay here for a while and keep Limpy company. I made that excuse because I wanted to talk to you.

'And Limpy doesn't like to be in here during the forenoon. He likes to get down to a certain coffee house and drink the beverage concocted by a lady friend. So, as soon as he felt the hour was right, the old reprobate asked me to stand in for him and went off to see his friend.'

Barney nodded. Pardoe, then, was a person of some influence. That much was obvious. The young man was still curious, but his eyes had strayed to the paper, and his thoughts turned to his losses of the previous night, in the fire. He remembered the sketches which had been destroyed and at once he knew what he must do before anything else.

'I wanted to see you about a business proposition. An assignment of work, exclusively for me, for which you would be well paid.'

Pardoe glanced anxiously into the cell, but his listener's attention had gone. Barney had propped the board up against the side wall of his cell and was in the act of smoothing a sheet of paper over it.

'You didn't happen to bring some nails, or anything with you?' he enquired moodily.

'No, I didn't, but there are some on this desk top. Here you are.'

The portly man carried them across and took with him a light hammer used for tacking reward notices to the walls. He handed the items into the cell and Barney at once set himself up to do a drawing. Pardoe hovered close, not sure whether his talk of a business proposition had been heard or not.

Barney started to outline a man's head and shoulders. They were not those of Pardoe, or anyone else in the town. Presently, the young artist turned to his visitor and contemplated his curious face.

'Mr Pardoe, I'm grateful to you, but before I can talk business with you or anybody else, there are things I have to do. Drawings. From memory. If you'd take yourself off now an' come back later I'd take it as a great favour. Will you do that?'

Pardoe was affronted. He wanted to show his annoyance, but the burning sincerity of the young man in the cell made him bottle it up and comply with the unexpected request. The ex-doctor sighed and backed away. He could not afford to rile the young man, if he hoped to get him to do a difficult job for him.

He retreated as far as the street door and watched for upwards of a minute. Barney had shut his mind to his surroundings, and also to the visitor. He was conjuring out of his memory the face of a man he had known well. Pardoe moved quietly out onto the sidewalk, unnoticed.

Barney made four sketches of the first man. The first was full face. The next two were in profile and the fourth showed the head tilted at an angle. He sighed a little and moved back a foot or more to contemplate his work. He seemed quietly satisfied and at the same time troubled.

He lifted away the top sheet and commenced work on a second one. Again he drew four sketches and the views were similar. As the fourth one was almost complete he kept glancing away towards the work on the first sheet, making comparisons.

A close observer of the drawings would have quickly concluded that the two men drawn on separate sheets were related. Each looked to be around thirty years of age and there were certain similarities of feature. They had barred brows, for instance, and short upper lips, and in profile it was clear that they both had craggy, bony foreheads.

The older of the two had a cleft chin, hidden in some sketches by a tuft of chin beard. In contrast, the other had a smooth chin, but he differed about the ears, having long pronounced lobes.

What the sketches could not show was the colour of their hair. In fact, the older one was a redhead and the other's hair was auburn.

Having finished the second series of drawings, Barney appeared to be drained of energy. He squatted back upon the bench and propped his chin upon his hand. His gaze slipped away from his work and he contemplated the floor, taking no account of a diamond of sunlight coming from his window.

★　★　★

Some ten minutes later, Doctor Pardoe encountered Dan Moore strolling watchfully along the sidewalk.

'Is Limpy busy in the office?' Dan asked without enthusiasm.

'As a matter of fact he's gone out to take coffee. But there's nothin' to worry about. Your prisoner is sketching in his cell. I wanted to ask you. Have you seen any more of the man who started the fight last night?'

Dan shook his head. He wondered why a retired doctor should be interested in such a happening. 'No, he's nowhere about. I've been to all the usual places a man might go to for a casual night's lodgin' an' there's no sign of him.'

'Do you think he was the one to start the fire? Was he capable of attempting to burn a man alive?'

Pardoe had lowered his voice so as not to be overheard, but he was serious enough, and his query left Dan with a knot of worry in the pit of his stomach.

'Fire-raisers are peculiar villains the way I see things,' Dan murmured. 'I don't like that sort of criminal. If Barney had to be disposed of, it could have been done with a gun or a knife. Fire is too drastic. I wouldn't like to think that we still had a fire-raiser hangin' around the town. It's convenient to think that the bearded man in the saloon might have done it, but, well, I don't know.'

The discussion might have pushed Dan's thoughts towards useful conclusions, but at that moment there was a diversion. Fifty yards down the sidewalk, a woman was calling to him. He turned and saw that it was Jenny Braid dressed for her daily exercise in horse-riding.

Dan nodded a kind of dismissal to Dr Pardoe and moved forward to meet

Jenny. Part of her anatomy strained against the neat blue shirt. Her face was flushed through running in riding boots. She held out her hand towards him, offering an envelope.

'Here, a letter for you, Dan. Left on the end of the bar some time this morning, or possibly last night. Sorry we can't talk longer. Unless I can persuade you to come riding with me?'

He thanked her for the letter, gave her a tight smile and shook his head. When he had to take up riding again, he might not look so good at first. Of all people, he wanted to avoid showing himself up in front of Jennifer.

'See you when you get back,' he called brightly, and turned his step towards the office.

Jenny hovered for a few moments behind him, hoping for more warmth before the parting. She was disappointed, and presently she trotted off back again, determined not to show it.

Dan got within ten yards of the office before his curiosity made him pause and open his letter. All it said on the outside was his name: Deputy Dan Moore. It was written with a blunt pencil.

Inside was a single sheet of unlined paper with some other, smaller pieces stuck to it. The lesser pieces were men's signatures and the first glance at them produced a new and gripping tension in him. He turned towards the wall of the nearest building and pored over the words.

We, the undersigned, know where you are, Dan Moore.

We intend to get you as soon as the Kid comes out of jail.

Signed: Nevada Tom. Bruce McGillie. Pierre Ludeau (the Corsican).

A warning. Blood will be shed in Conchas Creek unless you quit it and come out looking for us.

* * *

For upwards of two minutes, Dan was stunned with shock. When he finally moved away, he was still holding the paper out in front of him and two men who failed to get an answer as he went past thought he was possibly feeling ill.

5

He folded up the paper with a hand which was unsteady. So his past had caught up with him. A job unfinished was about to come back into his life. His former enemies were not going to allow him to forget them. They were bold, and they threatened violence. Their threats and their suggestions had his racing thoughts anything but coherent.

He pushed open the door of the office, saw that the occupier of the nearest cell was calm and at once stepped out again. He knew where to find Limpy and he made it to the coffee house in record time.

The woman behind the counter started to smile at him and to lift a coffee pot, but he almost ignored her, calling out to Limpy who was seated at a table in a secluded alcove out of sight from the street. The jailer, sensing trouble, came out of hiding and hurried to the door, achieving a bizarre lop-sided run.

'What is it, Dan?'

'Work, Limpy! Finish that coffee on the double. Collect food for that old drunk in the back corridor an' tell the other fellow I'll let him out as soon as I can get back. Understand?'

Limpy nodded unhappily. 'Yer, yer, Dan, right away. Are you goin' any-where special?'

'Nowhere special. I've jest got some walkin' and thinkin' to do. That's all. Get back there an' help me, why don't you?'

Dan withdrew, refusing the offer of fragrant coffee. He set off up the sidewalk with a distant look in his green eyes. He wondered how different he was now from the hard-riding sheriff's deputy who had ridden so fearlessly after desperadoes in Many Springs County.

He fought down the overpowering

anxiety which he had known since he opened the letter and tried to think constructively. For a time, he thought about how the letter had reached town. Almost anyone could have brought it. Its arrival did not necessarily mean that a member of the gang was in town. It might have been brought in by Barney's bearded stranger, or by anyone at all passing through.

The threats had to be taken seriously. Moreover, this was not a matter which he could make generally known. Marshman, the marshal, would be back in town any time, but he was not the sort of militant peace officer who would tell his deputy to stay put and who would offer assistance against the outlaws when they arrived.

Marshman, if he knew the contents of the letter, would expect him to move on. He might insist upon it, or have him relinquish his badge and then bring pressure upon him to move on.

Dan walked until he found himself outside a small Mexican *cantina*. He paused there, went inside and took coffee from a moustached proprietor who thought the deputy's presence gave his establishment a touch of prestige.

On this occasion, the peace officer did not avail himself of the opportunity to exercise his knowledge of Spanish. He was uncommunicative; almost aloof. He was going to have to face up to his own shortcomings. He would have to run out his horse and take some riding practice and find out for sure how his hip would stand up to punishing work on horseback.

He had to get back on a horse. A man on the move in that part of the world would certainly be vulnerable to his enemies if he could not sit a horse. He would be reduced to travelling on coaches or slower vehicles. As a hunter, he would be useless. And that was what he would have to become again. A mounted hunter of his enemies.

He tried to think of the situation in another way. Almost certainly people would be shot at if the Kid's men had the slightest excuse for coming to Conchas and making trouble. And there were many people in the town that Dan would not have subjected to such danger. Jenny Braid was prominent among them. He shook his head. If only he could have regained his confidence before this.

The coffee burned him as it went down. He wondered what his best course of action would be. Should he hand in his badge as soon as Marshman appeared, or should he hold on for a short while and try to get some practice in riding and shooting first?

He was still very much in doubt about his future course of action when he headed back for the street.

* * *

Limpy hurried about his chores when he returned to the office. He passed on Dan's message to the young artist, but that was poorly received because Barney had been awake long enough to have developed a healthy appetite.

In order to pass the time until the deputy's return, the prisoner in the office cell reached up to his window bars and chinned the sill several times to exercise his arm muscles. He was still busy when Dan came in and hurried across to him with the cell keys.

'Good day to you, Barney. I hope you've got over your rough time of last night. I can tell you that the bearded fellow is nowhere to be found. I've searched everywhere, and he seems to have cleared out. Don't waste your time lookin' for him. Go and get some food. Are you thinkin' of movin' on?'

Dan glanced curiously at the drawings which Barney brought out of the cell with him, but he did not ask any questions.

Barney reached the outer door. 'I'm a drifter, pure an' simple, Dan. Sure I'll be movin' on, but I could come back later if you want to talk to me about anything. I don't have any pressin' business waitin' for me.'

Dan warmed to the idea of a further discussion, and the two parted amicably. As soon as Barney appeared on the street, Dr Pardoe spotted him from a distance and they joined forces. Presently, in a clean eating house with a luscious smell of food, Barney began to satisfy his hunger. Opposite him, the older man sipped coffee and awaited his opportunity to say what he had wanted to divulge earlier.

Presently, his chance came. He pushed back his chair and fumbled in the inside pocket of his tailored coat. From a small wallet he produced three photographs, mounted on fairly stiff card. They were in black and white and had obviously been done by an expert photographer.

A young woman in her middle twenties had posed for them in a studio. She had long black hair down to her shoulders and worn loose so that it hung decoratively just wide of her oval face. In repose, her mouth looked small and firm under a strong straight nose, but in the photo where she smiled her expression was transformed. The mouth looked to be more in proportion and revealed small even teeth.

She had long sloping shoulders and a nicely rounded bust. Barney studied the photos across the table and his interest quickened. He pushed aside his plate and extended his hand, his face wearing an enquiring look.

'Are these photographs of your daughter, Mr Pardoe?'

The older man winced, and Barney saw at once that he had made a bad mistake. Pardoe shook his head. He explained: 'No, this is my wife, Margaret. You can't be blamed for falling into error. Most people seem to find it strange when one partner to a marriage is much older than the other.

'I admit to being over twenty years her senior. Now, having admitted that, I'd like to know what you think of her. Give me your opinion of her, now that you've seen her likeness. Feel free to be frank, otherwise I shall be insulted.'

Barney pushed his fingers through his unruly curls. He was acting almost as if he was in the presence of a strange lady. A glance at Pardoe's face confirmed that he wanted the truth, as revealed by the photos. The young man nodded. He set out the pictures in a line where his dinner place had previously rested.

'They were taken about five years ago,' Pardoe prompted.

Barney nodded. 'The rigours of life have not affected her appearance. I'd say that now she is probably about thirty years of age. She looks to me as though she might have been reared some distance away from here. What I mean is, she doesn't have the look of having been reared in a log cabin.'

'So far you are right. She was born back east, in Philadelphia. Her father was a lawyer who came out west and was disappointed with the sort of life it offered. But I may be putting words into your mouth. Please go on. I thought you were doing well.'

Barney licked his lips. All the time he was examining the pasteboards he was wondering what sort of a mystery lay behind them. In the ordinary course of events a man of mature years would not flaunt his young wife in front of a young and impressionable male stranger. He would not take that sort of risk.

Suppressing his burning curiosity, Barney resumed. 'What colour are her eyes?'

'Blue. Dark rather than the usual pale colour.'

'I find them very expressive, Mr Pardoe, a sure sign of character. I would say she has good taste, and a rather pleasing disposition. On occasion, however, she might appear to be very stubborn. She looks as if she has a mind of her own. Am I right?'

Looking hurt, Pardoe nodded. 'Unfortunately, yes. There have been occasions when she has made up her mind and nothing that I could do would make her change it. Do the pictures tell you anything else?'

Barney shrugged. He was reluctant to commit himself further. To break a growing silence, he smiled sheepishly. 'I would like to draw her likeness. Would that be possible?'

Pardoe leaned forward with almost pathetic eagerness. 'I was hoping you might say that. I wanted to ask you to do me one or two big drawings, take them from these photos. You could work from photos, couldn't you?'

Barney nodded slowly. 'Yes, of course, if you really want me to. A real life model would have been better, but you're the boss. You say what you want done. By the way, I enjoyed the meal. Thanks a lot.'

Pardoe snapped his fingers and the dirty plates and cups were taken away. As soon as the table was cleared, the drawing board was placed upon it, and Barney saw that he was to do his work on the spot. He had no objection, and he said as much.

The older man pushed back his chair and lit a cigar. He looked troubled at times, but he was obviously going to get a kick out of seeing the work done.

As always, Barney started slowly. He kept glancing from one small picture to another, sizing up the views as though he wanted to see his absent subject in three dimensions. When he started the first outline, the tip of his tongue was busy, exploring the edge of his lower lip.

Dr Pardoe was almost as intense as the artist. His gaze shifted from the drawing paper to the photos and then to the young man's animated face. Barney's expression was a study in itself. Sometimes he smiled a little. At other times he was intensely serious in outlook. After some ten minutes he straightened up and looked Pardoe in the face without seeing him. He then reapplied himself to his work and finished off the first effort.

As soon as he had done, he pulled the first sheet from the board and carefully passed it over. Pardoe made slight noises of delight. He was obviously pleased, and his enjoyment had a pleasant effect upon Barney who tried to think up a new angle for his second effort.

'You haven't done exactly what I expected, but I like it. Go ahead and do the same sort of thing again,' Pardoe suggested. 'I don't want to take up too much of your time, but I would like another. I'm assuming you don't have any urgent appointment anywhere.'

Barney nodded half-heartedly and set about the second picture.

'You saw at once that I had drawn her as she might be now. Five years later. I think myself that seen as she is in the picture, a little more mature, she is even more beautiful. Am I right?'

'I don't rightly know,' Pardoe admitted, with a beaten look upon his face. 'But I do like the way you've portrayed her. Maybe we could talk about her and the present on another occasion.'

The fingers of the artist were soon busy again. The first picture had shown Margaret Pardoe full face. This second effort showed her left profile, which

Barney had rightly guessed was her better one. Her chin was tilted up and her eyes were looking at something a few feet beyond the bounds of the picture at a slightly higher level. The suggestion was that she regarded a person, someone close to her in everyday life.

Pardoe groaned inwardly a couple of times as the second portrait was under way. Barney felt his inner sorrow, and at one time he wondered if he was doing the best for Pardoe by carrying out his wishes. The ex-doctor was almost acting as if his young wife was deceased. Barney wondered if this was the case, but he did not have the effrontery to ask. He put all he had into the second portrait and he felt somewhat lethargic and tired when it was completed.

Feeling the need to see things at a greater distance, he stepped to the window of the cafe and stared out into the street. Through the drapes no one could see him from the other direction. He closed his eyes, and in his mind's eye he could see Pardoe's wife walking around in an imagined room full of tasteful furniture. He wondered if Pardoe saw her that way, and he opened his eyes and turned towards him.

Pardoe was in the act of rolling up the two pictures. He did it with great reverence, as though they were newly acquired treasures. Barney returned to the table and collected his other pictures and the board and pencils.

'I've enjoyed your company, Mr Pardoe, and I hope you have some pleasure from the sketches. You and your wife, both.'

Pardoe winced as though he had been stabbed with a knife. He recovered his poise with an effort. 'Here, Barney. Here's ten dollars. I'm obliged to you. I don't feel as though I should take up any more of your time now. All the young are restless. I'm sure you're no exception. One thing more, if ever you feel like earning yourself a good deal of money, I have a project which might be to your liking. You'll think of me again, perhaps, before you move on?'

Barney said his thanks. They shook hands, and the artist promised to bear in mind what his benefactor had said. Pardoe got as far as the door. There, he hesitated as though he might have returned. Was he going to outline another scheme then and there? But no, again he changed his mind.

The ex-doctor stepped out into the street and walked off with his wife's likenesses tucked under his arm and held like a cradled weapon.

6

Around eleven o'clock Barney went looking for Dan Moore and found him quite elusive. He asked in two or three stores if anyone had seen him and then headed for Jenny's Place; Jenny claimed not to have seen him for some time.

At a few minutes to midday, a man who had been in the saloon the previous evening waved to Barney, and when questioned indicated the direction in which Dan had gone. The young artist discovered him sitting in the semi-gloom of the Mexican *cantina* and there he pulled up another stool and leaned on the bar.

'Howdy, amigo. You sure do know where to go when you decide to drop out of circulation. I think you must have something troubling you. Jennifer wanted to know if you had said anything about a letter she delivered to you.'

Dan shrugged, grinned, and asked in Spanish for a cool beer, which was quietly put beside Barney's elbow. They both drank from their glasses before the deputy made any attempt to satisfy the other's curiosity.

'I come here sometimes when I want to think. That letter I received contained threats from old enemies of mine. I have troubles jest the same as anyone else. In fact, their threats have put me in a curious position. They are a pretty deadly bunch. If I don't clear out of Conchas Creek and go lookin' for them, they have pointed out that the local townsfolk are likely to suffer.

'It's not a nice situation for a man who likes to make up his own mind. I won't ask you what you would do. It wouldn't be fair. Let's talk about you. You'll be movin' on soon. Did you have a satisfactory meeting with Victor Pardoe?'

Barney accepted the makings of a

cigarette and quietly enthused over the retired doctor. 'He brought me paper, pencils and a drawing board. And then he bought me food, an' all he wanted from me were a couple of sketches of his wife.'

As soon as Dan heard mention of Mrs Pardoe his interest quickened.

'You did sketches of his wife for him?'

Barney nodded. 'From three photos which he had with him.'

'Did he say why he wanted them?'

This query brought an odd look from the artist. 'Does a man have to give a reason for wantin' a woman's likeness? He wanted them because he is obviously deeply in love with her. He wants them for himself, of course! I guess that's the way things are with lovin' couples.'

'He needs the pictures of her because he no longer has the pleasure of her company. She walked out, or rather ran out on him about two years ago. He didn't have an inkling that she was unsettled, and jest about the time of a fair she disappeared while on a visit to town.'

Barney whistled. This explanation of Pardoe's married condition was very revealing. He brooded over what he had just learned for upwards of two minutes. 'And he's never seen her since?'

'No. If he had it would be all over the town. Pardoe would give anything to get her back, but no one knows quite where she is. There was a rumour that she had shown more than a passing interest in a fellow who came in for the fair. A stranger, he was. One of the type who can easily fascinate women. She might have gone off with such a fellow, but there was no evidence to substantiate the idea.'

Barney ended another brief silence. 'I wonder if she wants to come back to him?'

Dan gave a mirthless chuckle. 'You never can tell with women. They're so changeable. I'm sorry for Pardoe. So are most of the townsfolk, but me, I've got problems of my own. More pressing ones.'

Barney ordered another round of beer. When it was produced and ready to drink, he commented: 'My enemy, the one with the beard, has moved on.'

This time Dan nodded.

'While I was askin' around after you, I found out that he had headed away towards a ranch known as the Box T, located north-east of here. How does that sound to you?'

'I'd like to think you only have one enemy. That's to say, maybe the fellow who fought with you over his portrait also set fire to the shed, in an effort to burn you an' any more pictures you might have of him. If what you learned is correct, he's gone to the Tate place. Simeon Tate owns the ranch. He's as straight as any man. But he wouldn't have any reason to know the type of man he was dealing with this time.

'Maybe your bearded friend has gone after a job there.'

'If he has, I'll catch up with him. I owe him a few hearty punches, even if he was innocent of setting the shed on fire. I suppose you wouldn't entertain the idea of ridin' out there after him?'

Dan frowned. He felt that to expect such a course of action was asking a lot, and that Barney was expecting a lot after their brief acquaintanceship in suggesting such a thing.

'Now, how in the world do you come to think a thing like that? You ought to know that the town is my territory. I'd ride out beyond the town boundaries, of course, if the situation warranted it, but who's goin' to do a half day's ride out to a ranch on the offchance that a man might be a fire-raiser? If he did start the fire, how would I prove it?'

Dan sounded angry and bitter, and Barney felt sympathy for him. He toyed around with the rest of his drink, ground out his smoke butt and turned almost inevitably to his sketching materials. Dan watched what he was doing, and, because of his troubled thoughts, he felt he could do without a sketching lesson at this stage.

'I've got to be showin' myself. It ain't good, hidin' away like this when there's only that old jailer in the office. You'll have to excuse me. I know I haven't been very good company, an' I asked you specially to call back and talk.'

'Give me five minutes,' Barney begged.

Dan almost declined, and then gave in. He slipped back onto his stool and took a grip on his ebbing patience. The moustached proprietor showed much more interest as the newly sharpened pencil began to rough out a man's face on the paper.

As he worked, Barney talked. 'Have you ever thought about beards and facial hair?'

Dan did not answer, and consequently, the artist resumed. 'I mean that not all men who wear beards and moustaches do so to attract women. Neither do they do it to impress men. Some of them grow hair to alter their faces. Now, if you'll take a look at this outline, you'll see how my enemy would look without his beard. Don't let the eyes take all your attention. Have you seen anyone like that?'

Dan pushed back his hat and took a long look at the sketch. The bearded man looked quite appreciably different without the beard, but he was still a very homely specimen and a complete stranger in every way to the deputy.

Shaking his head, Dan said: 'I appreciate the object lesson you've given me, but he's still jest as much a stranger as he ever was. I'm sorry you've gone to all that trouble for nothing.'

He slipped off his stool, tossed a coin on the counter, and acted as though he was about to leave.

'An' you've never seen anything like him anywhere?'

Barney sounded very disappointed. Dan pondered over this new experience, and he failed to come up with anything different.

'What exactly are you gettin' at, amigo? Does your lesson have a special point to it?'

'Well, all the peace offices I've ever been in keep a heap of old reward notices. I thought you might have seen this man's face on one of them. It was jest an idea. Some of the men in the saloon say this hombre backed off mighty quickly when he saw your badge. I thought he was shy of the law. Forget it. I'm sorry to have taken up your time.'

Dan looked perplexed. He knew that quite a long time had gone by since he examined that particular collection in Marshman's office. He figured that he had deliberately put off the day when he would have to start chasing armed gunmen again. His shunning of the reward notices had something to do with his lack of confidence in himself as a horseman and a riding lawman.

'I must go back to the office an' take another look at the latest pictures of wanted men. You've touched my conscience, Barney. How about comin' back to the office an' takin' a look with me? I'm sure you'd be interested if the reasonin' behind your theory is correct.'

Barney, who had been feeling rather downcast, now brightened up considerably. He gathered up his belongings. He found that Dan walked so quickly on the way back to the office that it was difficult to keep up.

'If Westerners settled their differences on foot, you sure would keep clear of trouble, Dan,' the artist complained.

Dan peered over his shoulder and raised a smile for the first time in quite a while.

As soon as they were in the office, Dan was as businesslike as ever. He studied Limpy, who was poring over the articles in an old newspaper held about two feet away from his face. Limpy gave him a doubtful look and slowly lowered the news sheet.

'Something else cropped up?' he enquired cautiously.

'Nothin' for you to worry about, Limpy. How is that old fool in the back corridor?'

'He's come to his senses now, an' feelin' a bit sorry for himself. I told him what he'd done while under the influence of alcohol an' he didn't like what I had to say. His pardner, a man with a broken hat brim, came in askin' for him, too. I told him to wait down the street, an' keep out of your way 'cause you was still pretty sore about the whole affair. Did I do right?'

Dan, who was standing with one foot planted on a bar on the underside of an upright chair, nodded and grinned.

'I'd like for you to hustle him out with the smallest possible delay. Empty his gun before you give it to him an' advise him to move on. His next spell in one of our cells might cost him twenty-five dollars. You can see about that, Limpy? Barney an' me, we have a bit of private business to go into.'

'Oh, sure, Dan. It ain't no sort of a chore for an experienced fellow like me.

I'll have him out in no time.'

'An' when you've finished, go an' see if you can find a good cup of coffee for yourself. And drink it slowly.'

Chuckling with mirth, Limpy dropped the key ring. He retrieved it and went off into the cell corridor. Meanwhile, Dan had open the drawer where the notices were kept, and he produced a huge dust-laden handful and dumped them on top of the desk. He took the swivel chair and Barney carried over an upright.

'I can see why you wanted me to take a look at the notices,' the latter murmured. 'You could bind all this lot together an' make a book out of them.'

'There's been quite a lot of law-breakin' in this neck of the woods during the past few years,' Dan remarked, smiling broadly.

Abruptly, his expression changed. His thoughts had gone back to Kid Diamond and his boys, and the threat brought in by letter. Light perspiration beaded his brow. He pushed back his

91

hat, hoping that Barney would not notice how he was, and then took off his headgear altogether. So engrossed were the two searchers that neither of them looked up when Limpy and the prisoner, Zack, came out from the corridor on tiptoe and headed for the street door.

Limpy had done all his essential talking in the cell, and so nothing much was said in the office. Zack looked a little bit unsteady as he tiptoed the last yard or so to the door of freedom, but he reached it, and the only big noise he made occurred when he was through the door and closing it.

Dan glanced up. Limpy was hesitating before darting out to take more coffee with his lady friend. Zack went past the window, on the sidewalk, almost running. Dan lost interest at once, and Limpy took that as his dismissal. The door closed quietly the second time, and the turning over of the 'wanted' advertisements was redoubled.

Barney sneezed as dust attacked his

nostrils. He stopped for a few moments and blew his nose. Dan got on with his searching at a quicker rate. Every now and then Barney came upon a face the contours of which interested him as an artist and this made his progress slow.

The searching was more than half over and Dan was already trying to think up things to say to minimize Barney's disappointment when the notice they were looking for came up in Barney's pile. Barney stopped rather abruptly, but he said nothing. He was comparing the features of one Scarface Dick Petters with those he had drawn in the saloon the previous night.

The change in Barney at last communicated itself to the deputy who roughly pushed aside his own papers and grabbed for the vital one.

As his eyes roved the paper, he read aloud the words.

'Five hundred dollars reward for the capture of this alarming ruffian, Scarface Dick Peters. His face was scarred some years ago in a knife fight before he left the Texas Panhandle. He works alone, and when he gets short of funds he will rob and attack anyone who looks a likely victim. Beware of his knife and his gun. He uses both and is very ruthless. You have been warned.'

Dan broke off and looked up. Barney was grinning broadly. 'Maybe if you hadn't intervened when you did, he might have pulled a knife and attacked me with it! I was lucky to get off as lightly as I did, with only a bruised head. Now, how about comin' with me to that Box T place? I can sink a few punches into his dirty hide and then you can bring him in and claim the reward. I'll be good practice for you, amigo.'

The deputy did not react at first to Barney's advice and suggestions. His full attention appeared to be still centred on the notice.

He resumed. 'This reward is offered for his wrong-doings in Blackrock. That's away on the south-eastern boundary of this county. And ain't it strange, him havin' a jagged knife scar on his chin under that beard? Who'd have guessed, except maybe an artist?'

'All right, fellow, skip the compliments. When do we start out for the Box T?'

Suddenly the full purport of Barney's words became clear to Dan. He pushed the two heaps of notices into one pile and slowly rose to his feet. To a close observer such as Barney it became at once clear that he had blanched under his tan.

7

At one o'clock in the afternoon, Dan and Barney were mounted up on their horses outside the peace office talking to a tall thin Mexican with a bandanna wrapped rather tightly round his neck.

Valdez, the Mexican deputy who had been sick with a fever, kept massaging the cloth at his throat. 'Senor Dan, you don't seem to realize I still have these germs. I might give them to anyone who came along to the office an' that would not be good.'

Barney, looking very much at ease, mounted on his dappled grey stallion with his drawing board tied to his back, favoured the discomfited Mexican with a tolerant grin. Dan, mounted on his dun which had a splendid black mane and tail, also tried to sound tolerant, but he did not find it easy. His horse was not a particularly difficult one to handle. He simply lacked confidence on its back.

'Ain't nothin' much for you to do till the marshal gets back, Juan. No prisoners, an' everyone will get out of your way when you do the rounds 'cause they know you've been ill. So take it easy, huh? You can rest up most of the time in the office. Give the marshal my regards if he turns up before we get back.'

Valdez nodded rather furtively. 'Where should I tell him you have gone?'

'To the Box T ranch in search of an outlaw, name of Scarface Dick Petters. The reward notice is on the desk. *Adios.*'

This time the two riders really did make it away from the office, but there was another meeting before they could get clear of the town. At the west end of Main Street, they encountered two other riders coming in from the south-west.

Marshal Jabez Marshman had excellent eyesight for things seen at a distance. He partially checked the low-barrelled skewbald which he was riding and laid a hand on the shoulder of the stoop-shouldered young man riding beside him.

'Take a good look at these two riders comin' towards us, Clint. The dark haired one on the dun horse is my assistant, Dan Moore. Real good at his job, Dan is. Can't think why he'd be ridin' out of town when I've left him in charge, though.'

Clint Farr was just twenty years old; up from the country with his uncle and keen to settle in the town. He was about the average in height, leanly built with a lantern jaw and high arched eyebrows which gave the key to his somewhat ingenuous expression. Limp fair hair straggled from under his stetson, which was narrow-brimmed and undented.

'You think he'd take kindly to workin' with me, uncle?'

'I don't rightly know, Clint. Dan is a man you can think you know inside out, and then something happens an' he behaves in a way quite different from what you'd expect. He might take to you, an' then again he might not. You shouldn't worry your head about it, though, there's plenty of time to get him round to our way of thinking.'

Seconds later, Marshman was all smiles. He held his cylindrical body erect in the saddle as he raised his hand to his hat in a brief salute. Dan saw that he had grown a narrow, closely-trimmed grey moustache while he had been away. The shirt which showed beneath the buttoned vest was an unusual shade of brown. It was fastened at the neck under a string tie.

'Howdy, Dan? It sure is good to see you, you an' that friend of yours. This here is my nephew, my sister's boy, Clint, up from the country. He's thinkin' of settlin' in town an' seekin' out a job for himself.'

The marshal waited until the murmured greetings were over and then he broached the matter which was uppermost in his mind.

'Everything all right in town, no law breakin'? What's takin' you out on horseback, Dan?'

Dan nodded, acknowledging the question. 'There was a little fracas at the back of Jenny's place. Somebody set fire to that wooden shed with this hombre, Barney Malone, inside it.'

The marshal and his nephew showed a much greater interest in the lazy-looking fair-haired young man, but he looked away as though suddenly self-conscious, and Dan, who was not quite himself and more than a little impatient, resumed.

'No great harm done in the fire. Right now, we're ridin' to Tate's place in search of a man who might have caused the fire. One Scarface Petters, according to the reward document. You'll see it on your desk. You don't need to hurry. We'll see you when we get back, huh?'

Marshman nodded slowly as though

giving reluctant approval.

'Be careful how you go about it, Dan, especially if he's a fast gun. I wouldn't want to have you planted, not jest yet a while.'

'Don't worry, Jabez, I'm not ready for Boot Hill. So long, both of you.'

The two pairs parted and went their respective ways.

★　★　★

On the ride out to the Box T the pace was a slow one. Barney was at ease and quietly watchful. At times he was baffled when his slow striding stallion took the lead, and presently, Dan, who was coping at the easy pace, decided that he owed his partner some sort of an explanation.

'Before I took this job in town, I was a deputy sheriff elsewhere. After suf-ferin' a flesh wound at waist level I was caught off balance one day. When I hit the ground fallin' from the saddle I jarred my hip, an' that made ridin' rather difficult. I've kept out of the saddle on every possible occasion since because of the pain in my hip caused by the ridin' motion. Right now, I'm aware of my old injury, but the pain has not really shaken me.

'Sorry if I sound to be makin' excuses. I — er, I wouldn't have hesitated to come out ridin' after this jasper if it hadn't been for this old hip trouble.'

Barney sided him close. 'I knew you were workin' out some sort of a personal problem, Dan, but you don't have to be sensitive about it. Take your time, an' remember that when we get there, I'll be sidin' you.'

The two shook hands and the grip of friendship was a warm one.

Nearing the ranch buildings, Dan became alert. 'If Scarface has been taken on by the rancher, he'll be around that cluster of buildings or away to the north, on Box T range. If you like, I'll head straight for the house an' you can mosey over to the bunkhouse. That's the one, the long building over to the right. How'll that suit you?'

'It'll suit me okay, Dan. I'm still hopin' to tackle him with my fists before you take him in.'

Dan nodded. He reminded Barney what it said on the reward notice about Petters using a knife and a gun, and then he was bending to open the paddock gate. Once through it, they parted. Dan walked his dun towards the hitchrail fronting the galleried house, and Barney cut off towards the right, trying not to look too conspicuous.

Dan dismounted, holding his suspect hip as relaxed as possible. He mounted to the gallery and was met at the front door of the house by a pretty girl of seventeen. Lily Tate was generously rounded both above and below the waist. She was the apple of her ageing father's eye, no less.

Dan stepped back a short pace, as though bowled over by her femininity. There were slight smudges of dirt on her freckled face and she was carrying a

103

bucket of warm water. Putting down the bucket she waited to know his business. The visitor pretended to have a tickle in the throat to gain time. For the moment, Scarface Dick had been pushed to the back of his mind.

Lily draped herself against the door surround, and swung her hips provocatively. Her hair, golden in colour, was brushed back and tied at the nape of her neck in a green ribbon which matched her eyes. She had on a grey shirt and figure-hugging denims. A short black, bibbed apron did little to mask her shapeliness.

'So the law has caught up with the Tates at last. Good day to you, Dan. So nice to see you on a bright day like this, even if you do have a hacking cough. What can we do for you?'

The green eyes quizzed him. She was fully aware of the effect she was having upon him and she wondered how he would cope. Would he be tongue-tied, or was he sufficiently a man of the world to speak out and belittle his embarrassment.

'Doggone it, Lily, you're growin' up so fast a man can't rightly keep track of the shape of you.' Having uttered this much, he felt that his words had been ill-chosen, so he blundered on, sounding anything but happy. 'I'd like to say this was jest a social call, but it ain't. The fact is, I came lookin' for a man. One with a beard whose name is on a reward notice in the marshal's office. We thought he might be here, that your Pa might have given him a job?'

Lily forgot about her attractiveness for a few moments. 'You mean to say that homely-lookin' hombre, Richard Peterson, is actually wanted by the law? He *stole* something, maybe?'

'Is he here?' Dan persisted, fidgetting around at belt level.

'No, he's moved on, Dan. You're fresh out of luck. He didn't want a job. What he wanted was to change his horse. He had heard somewhere that Pa keeps more ridin' stock than he needs for his own use an' that's why he came here.

'He was ridin' a fine spritely sorrel when he arrived. It had plenty of bottom an' all the things that horsemen look for, but he had ridden it far too hard for ten days or more, so it wanted a long rest if it was ever goin' to give a good performance again.'

Dan shifted his weight from one booted foot to the other. Out of his eye corner he could see that Barney was coming back from the bunkhouse, leading his big grey.

'Who's your friend?' Lily enquired, suddenly full of interest.

'That's my buddy, Barney. But you were sayin'?'

'Pa did a deal with him. He took the sorrel an' let him have a black gelding about the same age and size. Peterson was a good judge of horse flesh. He was glad to have the gelding. He left a small amount of money to balance out the deal, too, although Pa thought he already had his money's worth when he gained the sorrel.'

'Hey, Lily! Ain't you ever comin'

back with that bucket? I could have been to the house an' back again three times by now, so hurry it up, will you?'

Lily pointed over her shoulder to where the two stables were, at the back of the house. 'Pa's in the stable with the sorrel right now, if you'd like to talk to him. He'd welcome your company, so long as you don't stop him in his work.'

Barney had hurried his step when he saw the pretty girl on the gallery. He took off his hat during the handshake, watched by two or three curious hands from the direction of the bunkhouse and the cook shack. Lily's curious glance made him slip the drawing board off his back and make an explanation of sorts.

Meanwhile, Dan took the bucket of water from the girl and set off for the stable with it. He was perhaps five yards away when Simeon Tate, a man nearing sixty in age, stepped out from the building in question and favoured him with a characteristic peering look.

Tate's grey hair was sparse on his

crown. He was long-faced with a drooping lifeless grey moustache and a squarely-cut grey beard. His peering look had started much earlier in life as a sun-squint. Now, however, his eyes were not so keen and he found that by half-closing them he could muster up a much clearer image. The sleeves of his soiled dun shirt were rolled up already, but he rolled them still higher when he identified Dan coming towards him.

'Land's sakes, there's no wonder an impressionable slip of a girl can't do a simple job when a handsome young peace officers struttin' around the yard! It was good of you to bring the bucket, Dan. Come on in here an' take a look at this sorrel. By the way, what can I do for you?'

'Good day to you, Simeon. I came lookin' for a fellow your daughter says calls himself Richard Peterson. He's wanted for a few crimes we don't talk about in front of ladies, an' I wondered if you could tell me where he might have headed for.'

The rancher, who was breathing hard after carrying in the bucket, whistled through his nicotine-stained teeth and sat himself down upon a three-legged stool which at other times was used for milking. He began to laugh almost soundlessly. Dan's earlier anxiety had faded. His mood matched that of the older man, but his attention was upon the sorrel for which the warm water had been brought.

'Doggone it, boy, you never can tell who you're dealin' with in this God-forsaken county an' that sure is the whole truth. You ain't here to tell me I bought a stolen horse, are you, Dan?'

Dan pushed back his hat and mopped his forehead. 'Come to think of it, Peterson wouldn't hesitate to steal a horse like that, if he felt like it. But I don't have anything to make me believe it is stolen, Sim, so there's no reason to question your ownership. Strange how some of these crafty characters go in for the very best in horse flesh.'

'All I can tell you about Peterson is

that when he left here he rode north over my land. Of course, he could have turned east or west an' I wouldn't know it, would I?'

His mood changed. He laughed gently and said almost reverently: 'This sure is a fine piece of horse flesh, ain't he now?'

Dan agreed wholeheartedly. He knelt beside his host and helped to mix a special type of powder into the warm water. This was some sort of a secret remedy Simeon knew about for taking fatigue out of a tired animal's muscles.

Between them, they rubbed the sorrel down with the liquid, and when they had finished they took turns with the grooming brushes to work on its hide.

★   ★   ★

Barney and Lily, who had struck up a friendship immediately, were walking side by side round the outside of the big high-fenced horse corral. Barney was explaining how someone had give him a pencil when he was a very small boy confined to his bed with a fever. He had started to draw at the age of five and had gone on ever since.

Their walking and talking was interrupted when Sim Tate and Dan came out from the stable, bringing the all-important sorrel with them, and put it into the corral.

Dan explained to Simeon who the fair-haired young man was, while Barney feasted his artist's eyes on the remarkable horse's lines.

'Why, that horse sure would look good if I could capture his outline on paper,' Barney remarked fervently.

'I'm sure Pa wouldn't mind if you wanted to draw him, Barney. Shall I ask him for you?'

Lily brought the four of them together and introduced the two men who did not know each other. She was particularly polite to her father, and as soon as the introductions were over, she explained that Barney was an artist.

Before the irascible old man could

ask what an artist was doing on his land, Lily had made the request on his behalf that the sorrel should be committed to paper. Noting the rancher's hesitation, Barney promised to leave the picture behind when he left the outfit, and that brought grudging consent from the owner.

Barney at once began to fix his board to the peeled poles of the corral, and Lily did all she could to help him. She was dancing about like a young fawn in spring when Simeon and Dan retired to the big general room at the front of the house.

For a time the conversation was about Barney, and then Simeon, who had stretched out on the settee to give his lower limbs a rest, steered the conversation round to something about which he was particularly curious.

'Let me see, Dan, you had some trouble with your back at one time, didn't you?'

Dan's hand went to his suspect hip. 'No, not exactly. It was my hip, Simeon.

Today has been rather an important day. I've been off the backs of horses for quite a while. I felt the time had come to try out my hip again, so I came this way to give myself a trial. So far, I've only had a few twinges, but you must take into account that my dun has not moved faster than a brisk walk. So I can't rightly say my old weakness is cured.'

Simeon commiserated with him, and the subject was changed.

8

Charlie Barrass was rather an unusual sort of chap for a Box T hand. He had worked for the outfit more than six years. At one time he had been a top hand, riding at point and planning the route for cattle drives with the ranch foreman. He worked really hard for long periods, but at the other times some sort of malicious streak in his nature put everyone against him.

He had demonstrated his skill one day in driving along a small bunch of beeves faster than any man in the crew could manage. Unfortunately, his feat of skill had gone out of hand and the fast driving had led to a minor stampede.

For this episode, he was reduced to working with the cook on the chuck wagon. Some time later, he had been operating as cook on another drive when an incident upset him. He reacted by driving the wagon at a breakneck speed until it overturned on the steep bank of a river.

Due to that incident and some others, Charlie had been confined to work around the buildings and on home range. How he had lasted for so long without Simeon Tate dismissing him was something of a mystery, but at thirty-four he was still very tough and capable, and there were many jobs around the ranch where his thick shoulder muscles could be put to good use.

Ever since the two riders had arrived at the spread, Charlie had been on the move between the stables, the smithy, the house and the bunkhouse. He had seen quite a bit of what had gone on when the visitors were out of doors and something about the way they were received made him want to create some sort of a diversion which would make the two visiting riders lose face in front of the Box T hands.

For several minutes, in between jobs, Barrass stood silently just within an empty stable, taking stock of what was going on near the big corral. As he watched, he smoked the stub of a cigar. His grey eyes were not wearing their innocent look and the way his thin mouth worked over his small sandy chin beard revealed much of his inner hostility towards his fellow men.

It was clear that young Miss Lily was involved with the artist fellow for quite some time. Barrass' thoughts turned back to the deputy marshal taking his ease with the master inside the house. He knew a few things about Dan Moore because when he went into town he made a crony out of Limpy Rogers, the jailer.

While under the influence of liquor, Limpy had revealed to Barrass that Moore was shy of horses, and had been for some time. Moore was the obvious victim. Anything to take a rise out of a peace officer was good for the morale. Barrass spat out his butt, killed it with his boot heel and slowly pulled a plug of chewing tobacco out of his trouser pocket. An ugly grin was spreading his stubbled cheeks.

Moore would make an interesting victim, particularly if a few of the workers around the buildings were there to see his downfall. It would have to look like an accident, of course. But that could be arranged. Barrass had once worked for a boxing booth and he knew quite a lot about underhand arrangements.

Barrass moved to the door. Hanging on nails above it was the article he had chosen for his little 'incident'. It was a short whip, made out of the skin of a rattlesnake. The rattle was still available should it be required. Barrass reached up and lifted it down, rolling it up small and stuffing it down his shirt. He stepped out into the open, watchful for any sign of movement from the house and started to make his presence known and felt to anyone who happened to be around.

In order to stir people up he whistled lively tunes and when he could he transferred buckets, brooms and sacks from one building to another. A score of hens, placidly clucking and pecking for food, were chased out from under a small hut on low stilts and made to scamper about in the open.

A dog started barking, and two horses, still in a stable, started to add their quota to the general noise.

Dan Moore emerged some ten minutes after Barrass had formulated his plan. Dan walked the length of the gallery with the owner at his back. From the corner of the building he peered in the direction of the corral and noted that Barney was still very busy.

'I won't wait for Barney, Sim. He can come along later. You'll find his drawing of that horse will be a truly great likeness. An' don't rush him is my advice. Lily won't come to any harm while he's around. You get back indoors an' take your ease, hear me? I'll jest mosey along back to town an' see if

Jabez has thought anything about work while I've been away.'

The two men shook hands, and the rancher said he was sorry that the outlaw fellow had gone on before he could be apprehended. Dan said it was the way of things. He mounted up, touched his hat to Tate, and unhitched the dun. Simeon hovered towards his front door and slipped indoors at the earliest possible moment.

Dan gave a distant wave to the young couple by the corral and looked away again. His head was lowered and his eyes in the shade as the dun walked placidly back towards the five-barred gate of the paddock.

Barrass appeared to come from nowhere. It was clear to anyone who followed his actions that he was supposed to be rounding up hens which were far too scattered. He came round a building clapping his hands and shooing some six or eight of the frightened birds along in front him.

Dan looked up, blinked and took no

further notice. Barrass arranged to go quickly behind him, and when he was in that position he brought out the rattlesnake skin whip and used it to great effect. The dun, however, was much more startled by the sudden rattling in the tail than any of the poultry.

The horse bucked and plunged and whinnied in fright, but Barrass — apparently without noticing the effect he was having — followed up closely, still cracking his whip and putting the dun into a terrified gallop straight at the gate.

Dan saw his problem quite clearly. He tried to restrain the animal but the distance was small and the time in which he had to act was negligible. Perhaps ten or fifteen seconds elapsed during which he knew that his suspect hip was about to have the father and mother of a testing.

This was the time of revelation. Either he would stay with the animal and his weak hip would take the added strain, or he would be thrown out of the saddle by the return of his old ache and the attendant strain. Although he was in the grip of a very real fear, he heard himself making the encouraging noises as of old, urging the dun to make a clean leap and clear the gate.

Dan's heart thumped. He knew that several men and perhaps two women were watching his performance somewhere behind him. He set his teeth and waited. To him, it seemed that the straining dun had gone too close before taking off in its leap, but the beast rose into the air, moving cleanly and with far more confidence than its master.

The rear hooves clipped the top rail of the gate and then they were clear. Dan positioned himself carefully, back slightly arched, feet braced in the stirrups. On impact, a slight tremor or twinge ran up from the base of his back to waist level. He waited for other developments and none came.

The dun took thirty yards to slow down, and then he turned it. He knew the identity of the man who had made them jump. A quick study of the situation and certain little things that he had gleaned from Limpy made him sure that it had been done on purpose. Barrass had sought to humiliate him, knowing his weakness.

And, fortunately, the humiliation had turned out for the best. Dan now knew more about himself, and what he had just learned boosted his confidence as nothing else had done in the past two years. He was ready to strike back, but how was it best to take his revenge without overstepping the mark?

His questing eyes looked for and found Charlie Barrass. The latter had been most amazed when his ruse failed to work. Surprised in his turn, he had failed to take himself off out of sight. Now, he hovered between the small stable and the main building. Dan remained beyond the gate, but he waved to the bearded man and called to him.

'Ho, there, Charlie, did you get all

your chicks together?'

Barrass put up his two hands to the rolled and pointed brim of his hat, an unconscious habit when he was unsure of himself. He glanced to one side and then to the other. His workmates were expecting him to make some sort of a reply. They knew him well enough to perceive that he had tried something a little bit underhand which had failed.

'Eh, well no, deputy. It seems they're well an' truly scattered today. Maybe I'll have to get a net to catch them all. Sorry if I startled your horse jest now.'

Dan leaned on his saddle horn, nodding easily. 'What's that on the heel of your boot, Charlie?' he asked, sounding suddenly serious.

'What? I don't see anything!'

Barrass was acting as though Dan's remark was a serious enquiry. He bent down and examined one of his boot heels. There was nothing wrong with it except that it was slightly worn down.

'Not that one. The other,' Dan prompted.

Barrass stuck out his other leg behind him and looked back over his shoulder to examine it thoroughly. He had no inclination at all as to what Dan was about to do. The deputy had all the time in the world to pull his gun, line it up on the boot heel and pull the trigger.

The aim was a good one, and the worn heel was blasted away from the rest of the boot while the owner continued to pose. He jumped, swore and started to reveal his inner anger. All around him, however, men were chuckling. Even a plump Mexican female servant was laughing so hard that she might have burst her outer garments. Barrass thumped one fist into the other hand. He turned on his heel and hurried off to the stable, which had been his earlier vantage point. His walk was rendered rather difficult and a further source of merriment because of the missing heel.

Dan called: 'Be seein' you, Charlie!'

He waved his hat to all who were watching, including the freshly-emerged rancher, and went off at a brisk canter, whistling to himself and feeling on top of the world.

★ ★ ★

Barrass awaited his chance to make some sort of a move against the lazy-eyed young man who had drawn the horse. Barney was indoors along with Lily and her father for upwards of half an hour while the two Tates admired the drawing and gave him some light refreshment.

At last, young Malone came out, beaming all over his youthful unlined face and promising that he would call again, if he remained for any length of time in the district. His grey had been moved. While they said their farewells, Barney's shaded eyes were busy. He had witnessed part of the exchange between his friend and Barrass.

Now, he was curious to see that Barrass had taken his horse to a trough in order to give it water. He was thinking that Barrass was watching every move the visitors made. Here he was, just bringing the horse, all ready for mounting and taking away. Could he be up to some further mischief?

Lilly and Simeon remained on the gallery, while Barney walked a few yards towards the fence where the big gate was located. As Barrass came towards him from the trough, leading the grey, it was very obvious that he had taken off the boots he had been wearing. In their place he had donned a pair of mocassins.

When the two men and the horse came together, they were sufficiently far away from the house for their conversation to be out of earshot.

Barney looked the horse over. While Barrass waited expectantly, the artist noted that the saddle blanket had been rumpled, and that the grey was looking distinctly ill at ease.

He said over his shoulder: 'What is it this time, Barrass? A burr under the blanket?'

In spite of his self control, the bearded man gasped. His ruse had been seen through far too readily. He protested.

'Aw, shucks, man, jest because I have a little fun with old Dan, you have to think the worst of me. Why should you? We ain't met before. I ain't got any reason to interfere with your property, have I? I was only tryin' to do you a favour.'

'Then mount up first and prove I'm wrong in my guesswork,' Barney suggested, in a clear voice which carried.

'You ain't serious, are you?'

'Mount up, an' make it snappy, amigo. I don't have all day to wait. This horse gets short tempered real easily, too. I wonder how you'll cope without boots or spurs? Are you going' to accept my challenge?'

Suddenly, Barrass lost control. He ran at Barney who had to turn quickly and fend off two haymaking swings. The artist stepped back. His eyes sought the expression in the other's.

There was no mistaking the viciousness motivating the bearded one. It was clear by the way he handled himself that he was a fist fighter, too. If he knew sufficient dirty tricks used in a boxing ring, he could win this contest without actually trying. Barney thought hard.

'Dan was right. There's something wrong with your foot.'

Barrass eased off in his charge. His eyes showed that his brain had registered the remark, but he did not look down. Barney hit him hard between the eyes while he was still, and then stabbed a boot on the nearer of the two mocassined feet.

Barrass winced and groaned. Barney caught him with a back-hander. A neat trip, and a punch to the waist line finished a contest which might very easily have gone the other way. Barrass folded up like a jack-knife.

Although he was breathing hard, Barney managed to hoist him up and drag him as far as the trough. As soon as they reached it, the trouble-maker was dumped in it. A few gallons spilled over, but the victor paid no heed. He returned to his restless mount and patiently stripped off the saddlery until he found the burr under the blanket and removed it.

As he rode away, some of the watchers gave him a ragged cheer. What pleased him most was hearing the girl's voice raised among the others.

9

Barney overtook his riding partner some two miles nearer town. Dan and the dun came out of a clump of dense grass, ran straight at a stream about eight feet wide and jumped it as if it were an everyday occurrence.

'Holé!' the artist yelled. 'Now jump it back again!'

Without waiting for a response he turned his own magnificent grey towards the water and made the jump in the opposite direction. Dan, looking very youthful and singularly free from cares, jumped it after him. They made another two jumps each before resting up to give the horses a breather.

They slackened their saddles and rocked them, leaving the horses to wade into the stream and drink. Side by side, the two men lay prone with their faces at water level. In between drinks,

Barney showed his admiration in words for what he had seen of the exchanges between Dan and Charlie Barrass.

Dan was greatly uplifted by the way his trial had gone, and he almost missed seeing Barney examining his knuckles which were reddened by the fist fight.

'Don't tell me you've been in action as well?' Dan queried. 'Not with Charlie again?'

Barney nodded. He took quite a bit of pleasure in explaining how the fist fight had been started. The brief bout had excited him and imprinted itself upon his memory. He recounted it, blow by blow, and enjoyed the reaction in the deputy, who regarded Barrass' second setback as an added pleasure.

They rolled cigarettes and smoked them before thinking of moving on again. When they were mounted up, about half a mile went by without any conversation. Each remained thoughtful without feeling shut off from the other.

Eventually, Barney cleared his throat. 'Judgin' by the way you were puttin' that cayuse over the water back there, you haven't had any bad pains due to your ridin'. That sure is an achievement, if I can say so without givin' offence.'

'It sure is an achievement. The happenings of today are goin' to materially change my life. I'm glad to feel competent in the saddle again because it has been clear to me since I got that threatening letter that I've got to hit the trail, even if only for a while.

'I've got to pit my wits against some old enemies, whether I like it or not. Besides, I couldn't stay in Conchas an' risk bringin' trouble to a whole lot of decent people. I guess I'll have to tell old Jabez some time tonight. He deserves to know the worst, don't you think?'

Barney nodded gravely. 'Do you have any particular place to ride to when you leave here?'

'Unfortunately, I have to find the Diamond boys by trial and error. I guess I might as well start off in the direction Scarface Petters took. I don't reckon he'll be easy to overhaul, but you never can tell. He might get careless, an' the reward for him is worth havin'. What will you do? Folks like you in the town. You could make quite a few honest bucks with your drawin' talent.'

Barney shrugged. 'It's a sensation with most people, seein' a face reproduced on paper. But the interest passes. Besides, I'm a travellin' man, myself. I haven't had a lot of experience of stayin' in one place. I'll be movin' on, maybe tomorrow.'

The incidents at the Box T seemed to have drawn the two young men together. Dan was thinking that when he rode out to do battle with his outlaw enemies, he would miss Barney — in spite of only a brief acquaintance — as much as he missed most of the townsfolk.

In fact, when the deputy examined his own feelings more deeply, Barney was ranged close behind Jennifer in his private thoughts. He marvelled at the change in his own attitude. At one time, he had regarded Barney as an interloper into the friendship between Jenny and himself. Now, after seeing how Barney got on with Lily Tate, that earlier feeling of disquiet seemed to have faded altogether.

He no longer felt that they were rivals.

* * *

The clock with the loud tick and the cracked face showed a little after six o'clock that same evening when Dan entered Marshman's office and found the stocky peace officer filling the old swivel chair.

Marshman looked up, saw who it was, and turned up the brim of his hat, as though by so doing he could see better.

'Howdy, Dan? Anything to report about that fire-raiser you went after?'

Marshman peered hard at Dan, as though trying to read his thoughts. Dan

134

waited until he was seated on an upright chair, some three feet away.

'No, the outlaw wasn't there. He'd changed his horse for one of Simeon's stock an' ridden off for the north, over Box T territory. I don't figure he'll be back this way, an' maybe that's a good thing, Jabez.'

'Maybe it is an' maybe it isn't,' the marshal murmured. He was not quite making sense, and the reason for that was something on his mind. 'Did you happen to see that nephew of mine, Clint, along at the eating house?'

Dan shook his head and tactfully waited to hear what it was that his senior had in mind.

'I thought it might have been a good thing if the two of you got to know each other, Dan. You see, I've taken over the responsibility for givin' that boy a start in life. In this town, in fact. What I really want is for him to take a job with us, workin' out of this office.

'If you took him around with you, you could show him how to handle himself in the sort of situations we have around here. Put him wise to the best way to handle drunks an that sort of thing. How would you feel about takin' on Clint's trainin'? Would it appeal to you?'

'Do you think he's the right sort of man for the job?' Dan asked carefully.

'I would say so, Dan. After all, he comes of the same sort of stock as I do. What do you think yourself?'

Dan shrugged. 'The fact is I'm not sure, but I don't want the job of trainin' him, Jabez.'

The marshal, who was easily affronted, showed his displeasure.

'Now why in the world are you sayin' no, young fellow? Let me remind you that I've done you favours in the past. Your reason has to be a might good one, or it won't wash with me. So what is it?'

'I have to ask for two weeks leave of absence to go man huntin'. And it has to be straight away.' Dan surprised himself by his own calmness. 'Believe me, Jabez, I haven't forgotten your kindnesses in the past.'

Jabez massaged his somewhat fleshy face. Dan's moderate tone had not entirely mollified him. He resumed. 'I told you, I've taken on the task of givin' this young nephew of mine a start in life. If it's Scarface an' reward money you're after there'll be other opportunities. Doggone it, the west has plenty of outlaws, active an' otherwise. You'll get your chance to tangle with road agents again. All I'm askin' you do is wait for a while — until I get young Clint established.'

Dan sighed. He dipped into his pocket and produced from it the threatening letter. While his steady fingers smoothed it out, he remarked: 'I know there are other outlaws on the prowl, Jabez. Perhaps if you read this you'll understand.'

The marshal seemed surprised. He took the paper, looked his deputy carefully in the eye and then spread it out in front of him on the desk. Tilting back his head to get it into better focus, he then began to read. Dan, by this time, knew the contents off by heart. He was able to say the sentences over in his thoughts while he watched his senior's complexion change.

Marshman jerked his shoulders and looked up. 'These, these are fancy names. How do you know it ain't all a hoax?'

'Because I've tangled with all those men before, an' the man referred to as the Kid as Kid Diamond. He's due out of jail almost at once. As soon as he joins up with the others, a reign of terror is due to start.'

Jabez began blinking rapidly. 'You really think they'd come to Conchas jest to get even with you?'

'That's no idle threat, amigo. So you see, I need two weeks off. Maybe more. This is your chance to bring your nephew into service. Give him advice yourself. Who is better qualified to do that?'

The marshal was nodding but his

thoughts were still upon the other issue, the outlaws' menace. 'You don't look like a man who specially wants to do battle with outlaws. I guess you must be movin' out to protect others. Am I right?'

'Absolutely, Jabez. Besides, if I stayed I'd be a sitting duck here. If I move on a bit, I might manage to spring a surprise or two when they go into action. If you like I'll do some patrollin' this evenin' but tomorrow I want to feel free. My preparations are not very elaborate, but I have to say a few farewells. All I can tell you is that I'll be travellin' north first. I wish you well with the trainin' of your nephew.'

Marshman came clumsily to his feet. He had been shaken almost as much as Dan had by the contents of the letter. Now that he was wise to Dan's intentions and his underlying motives, he was only too glad to accede to his wishes.

They shook hands and the older man moved out to go in search of food.

Dan was up shortly after dawn. Over a late night drink, he had furnished Jenny with some of the details of what had happened out at the Box T. She had seen the way he looked when he spoke of his being forced to do a big jump on horseback and no one needed to explain to her about the change in him. But his underlying worries were still with him and when he intimated that he had to go out of town for a week or two she feared the worst.

Barney had been and booked a room earlier, but he had gone on a ride out of town after that. Had he been around, Jenny would have asked him more about Dan and his plans. As it was, she had to retire to her bed with a mind full of conjecture and foreboding. She had a feeling that Dan was going to ride out of her life, now that he had his confidence back about horse-riding.

She surprised him as he left his room the following morning by appearing fully dressed on the upper landing as he tried to slip away to take his breakfast.

'Howdy, mister!' she called gaily. 'Do you have the time to take a short ride with a lady before you go out of town?'

Dan paused on the stairs and admired her. She had on a wide-brimmed cream coloured hat and a fringed riding shirt. Her brand new denims were tucked into expensive half boots. The long brown hair was hidden in the hat. He fought against his great longing to go riding with her.

'No, Jennifer, I really don't have the time today, but I promise to go ridin' with you the day I get back, provided it's not too late.'

They came down the staircase side by side and made an attractive couple. On the sidewalk they talked of everyday inconsequential things. All too soon, Dan reached for her and kissed her lightly on the cheek.

'Take care of yourself, Jenny,' he murmured.

The young woman's eyes were moist

as she murmured a similar reply. She turned and hurried towards the livery then, while Dan penetrated the steamy interior of the eating house. He was still breathless and a little downcast because of the parting when he encountered Barney sitting at one of the tables near the far end.

'I've been savin' this place for you, Dan. Couldn't think what time you'd be around, so I've eaten already. If it's all the same with you, I'll drink coffee till you're ready to leave. I thought we might ride north together.'

Dan tossed his hat onto the nearest rack and happily flopped into the chair which Barney pulled out for him. 'I sure will be glad of your company, Barney, but do you have any special reason for goin' north right now?'

A waitress came. Dan gave his order and the conversation was resumed.

'Sure. There's forty dollars of Vic Pardoe's money lurin' me away to search for that pretty wife of his. Is that reason enough for you?'

Dan drummed with his fingers on the table. 'Why did Pardoe choose you an' not an ordinary detective to do his lookin' for him?'

'Because he thinks that as an artist I'm more than passin' observant. Besides, what I've seen of his wife in photos interests me. He knows that. And in any case, I'm a natural born searcher. I haven't mentioned it before, but for years now I've been searchin' for my missin' kin. So it doesn't seem strange to me to take on another job of lookin' for people.'

Clearly, Barney was sensitive about his missing kin. For once, the ingenuous, almost lazy look was missing from his eyes. Dan found himself wondering how long they would stay together before their separate tasks drew them apart. He also wondered if he, himself, could do better at looking for missing people than Barney.

Presently, he shrugged. 'Well, I wish you joy in your searchin', Barney. The first thing that entered my head when you said you were ridin' north was that you were searchin' solely for that Scarface fellow, Petters. It's true we might encounter him, but bounty huntin' for its own sake does things to a man. I wouldn't advise you to take on that sort of work jest for the money reward.'

While Barney was thinking over his answer, Dan's food arrived, and that terminated the exchanges. They left town an hour later, riding side by side, and drawing many puzzled glances from lookers-on who had no inkling of their business.

10

There was no town in Santa Fe county directly north of Conchas Creek, but the partners rode more or less in that direction for a day and a half and then veered a little to westward to try their luck in the nearest settlement of any size.

The town was Redrock Wells. It was somewhat smaller than Conchas and there was far less activity about the streets. Some ten years earlier Redrock had flourished but that was before a cattle pest known as the Spanish tick had driven certain wealthy ranchers to seek pastures new.

Dan and Barney parted company after taking a late breakfast in the first café they encountered. Dan went looking for Scarface and Barney took some small sketches of Mrs Pardoe in the hope that someone might recognize her.

Dan's search was a tedious one which produced no worthwhile results. He made his way into all the public places without achieving anything and when he conversed with the local marshal, an ageing lugubrious individual who thought of nothing but whiskey and an easy existence, he received no help and no good wishes.

The deputy felt that Scarface had not come as far as Redrock, and that, as far as Dan was concerned, did not greatly matter. He then slowed down and took his ease in the bars, dropping an odd name here, making a comment there, hoping to get some sort of a hint as to whether the Diamond gang was known in the town, or was expected.

Again, he learned nothing of an informative nature, and presently he went in search of his riding partner.

* * *

Dan cut short his wanderings, and seated himself on a bench outside the most central of the saloons on Main Street. He was wondering how Jennifer was getting along when his elusive partner came striding up the sidewalk from the eastern end of town. It was clear at once, due to Barney's expression, that he had been more successful in his enquiries.

As the young artist reached him, Dan asked: 'Do you want a beer?'

Barney nodded. 'I've got the father an' mother of a thirst, but I must tell you what I've found out first. I met a man down there who didn't have his coach fare to the next town. He studied my pictures of Mrs Pardoe, and he told me that my missin' kin was now Mrs Diamond, the wife of a saloon keeper who lives in the next town west of here, a place called Ford. He was absolutely sure, so I gave him a golden eagle for his trouble. I hope I did right.'

Barney's troubled face seemed rather out of character to Dan, who thought that he had little to worry about, seeing that the ten dollars would come out of the expenses money provided by Vic Pardoe.

Dan gripped his friend's forearm. 'Did you get any details about this Diamond, the man she is said to have married? I have to ask you this because my old enemy's name is Diamond. He's known as the Diamond Kid, or Kid Diamond.'

Barney shook his head. 'This is not Kid Diamond. He is called Johnnie Diamond, though, an' he claims to be Kid Diamond's brother. My informant told me all I wanted to know, but he warned me to stay away because anyone who tangles with the brother of a bank robber is askin' for trouble.'

'You've brought me luck,' Dan murmured, with a grim smile. 'Our first clue, yours and mine. An' what's more, although our aims are different it looks as if we are to keep company for a day or two more. How do you feel about that?'

'I welcome it, Dan. Until I met you, I often felt lonely. Now, I hope the day is a long way off when we finally have to part company. Right now, I can think of nothing but my thirst. But this afternoon, when the heat is fadin', after we've eaten food, I'd sure like to be movin' on again. What do you say?'

'I'll be ready to move on when you are, pardner. So let's go an' see about slakin' your thirst.'

★ ★ ★

Johnnie Diamond, proprietor of the Dime saloon in the township of Ford, was a troubled man. Five or six years earlier, if anyone or anything had threatened his immediate source of income, he would have moved on and accepted the change stoically, but now, at the age of forty-two and with his establishment doing lucrative business, he did not want to move on. Moreover, he was scared.

For twenty years he had made his living as a gambler on river boats, as a confidence trickster and as an opportunist, walk-in thief. Now, however, he was established in one place with a business he had built up for himself; one which he did not want to sell or to cede to anyone else.

And there was Margaret. Five years had elapsed since he ran away from Conchas Creek with the restless wife of Dr Victor Pardoe. There had been times during that period when Johnnie had been unfaithful to her, but she had never shown any inclination to leave him, and for that he was grateful. She had brought a basic feeling of stability into his life which he had never known before. And now the life they had together was undoubtedly being threatened.

At ten in the forenoon, he rose from the smart padded chair which he used in the office at the rear of his saloon and strolled to a wall mirror which reflected his head and shoulders. Since he had settled down in Ford, he had lost some of his good looks.

His swarthy, handsome face had thickened out so that he had the beginnings of a heavy jowl forming from one side of his jaw to the other. Under the belted brown coat and trousers he was putting on weight. His tailor now found it hard to hide it. His dark hair, parted in the middle, was thinning at the temples and the crown. He could see lamplight through it.

He had puffy bags under his bulbous, lined eyes. His thin, bristling moustache adorned his upper lip like a third eyebrow and did little to enhance his appearance. He blew out his cheeks and exhaled in a long sigh. On the desk, the butt end of a cigar was slowly burning itself out. He emptied a glass of whiskey which had been filled up several times since he came into the office from his breakfast.

He slumped into his chair again. What he was feeling was insecurity. He had heard that his brother, the Kid, was due out of the penitentiary located in Socorro, and he — Johnnie Diamond

— knew better than anyone else that there was no blood tie between them. In fact, the only connection between himself and the outlaw was the name, the pretended relationship assumed only to boost business in the early days of the Dime saloon.

Johnnie had deliberately given himself notoriety, and now he lived with the fear of having to pay for it. The Diamond Kid would certainly have heard about the man who said he was his brother, and — being in a mean mood following his discharge — anything might happen. A liquored wanderer in the bar had one night given Johnnie the jitters by telling tales of how the Kid worked on his victims with knife and gun. The Kid was said to kill without compuction, if the occasion arose.

Margaret, at this time, was at the Diamonds' hideaway cabin, two or more miles north of Ford. Margaret was the real owner of the place. She looked upon it as her retreat. In order to keep her, and keep her interested in him and his doings, Johnnie had from time to time spent a great deal of money in furnishing the cabin.

The inside of it was very different from the exterior. He had had the walls skimmed and rendered smooth. Furniture of Margaret's choosing had been brought in by wagon from places much further east. The walls were hung with pictures of her choice and shelves down one wall held several hundred books.

Margaret was the daughter of a professional man from the east coast. One of the things about Victor Pardoe which had attracted her was his background. Pardoe was a man of some culture, well read and able to talk about books and history. At times, Pardoe had bored her, but the part of her make-up formulated by her early background and education still persisted after her flight to Ford.

Johnnie Dimes (this was the name on his birth certificate) had ditched a lot of women in his time, but Margaret was different. He wanted his life to go on as it had been in Ford, and Margaret was an essential part of it. And now she was still away at the cabin. In fact, she should have been back the day before. He never gave her orders or instructions as to when she should be back, but on this occasion he was worried. He had to admit to himself that the Diamond Kid business was getting him down.

Abruptly, he rose to his feet and entered the smoky, beer-laden atmosphere. Some of his old cronies noticed him at once, but the black look on his brow and the sourness of his utterances quickly made them think that his liver was playing him up.

In their opinion Johnnie Diamond was not the light-hearted character he had been a year or eighteen months earlier.

★ ★ ★

The searchers rode in from Redrock Wells some eight hours later. Neither of them went out of their way to make their business known to the people they mixed with. A half hour in the Dime saloon revealed that the Diamonds had a shack out of town, in a valley further north.

The tipsy character who provided this information explained that the owner was in a bad temper because the wife was away at the cabin on that very day.

Dan, who was passing himself off as an ordinary traveller, bought the barman a drink. As he paid, he asked: 'Is the owner around at this time of the evenin'? I heard tell he was something of a character. I'd like to talk to him.'

The barman stroked his freshly shaved chin. 'The fact is, mister, I can't really say if the Boss will show up tonight. At the moment, something's troublin' his liver. He tends to keep out of the bar when he's like that.'

Dan shrugged and grinned. When their glasses were empty, the partners strolled out into the open air. After a brief discussion, they decided to take a meal before making any further enquiries. They ate heartily, and Barney revealed his innate enthusiasm for the search as the food was consumed.

Dan smiled to himself and marvelled at the progress his buddy had made in so short a time. In comparison his own efforts had been feeble. Moreover, this kind of investigation could only lead him into deep and possibly lethal difficulty. He found himself tensing up as he thought about it.

Around seven-thirty in the evening, they parted company and went their separate ways, hoping to learn a lot more before they turned in for the night.

Acting on a hunch, Barney chose a rival saloon to make his further enquiries. The Bonanza was rather a dilapidated place and its clients did not appear to have as much money to throw about, but the proprietor, a man who grudged Johnnie Diamond his success, was eager to talk about his competitor in business.

Over three fingers of whiskey, bought with Pardoe's search money, Luker, the owner, talked of his palmier days when he travelled the trails with a salesman's wagon. He kept looking into the middle distance and finger-combing his brown moustache and beard, as he talked, and once in a while he lifted his expensive flat-crowned hat and stroked his bald head.

'Diamond's doing well. Have you ever been out to that private shack he keeps out of town?'

This enquiry brought Luker down to earth with a bump. He gave his questioner a hard, shrewd look, as though the query had lowered his opinion of him.

'Ain't that sort of a silly question to ask? Do you know anybody other than Diamond himself who has been asked out there?'

Barney flashed his ingenuous, disarming grin. He patted Luker on the shoulder and told him not to be so taken aback. On the table between them was a pile of coins, the change out of the second of Vic Pardoe's golden eagles. The young artist allowed his rather compelling blue eyes to rest upon it. Luker wondered what he had in mind.

'Me, I'd like another whiskey. So would you, Mr Luker. After that, I'd be willin' to part with all the money left on the table for a bit of information. I need to know the exact location of the Diamonds' out-of-town cabin.'

Luker whistled. He signalled to his man to refill the glasses and at the same time studied Barney's face. The frank blue eyes did not hint at any ulterior motive. This was hardly the gaze of a thief, for instance.

Luker stayed pensive. 'Now see here, mister. I don't have any reason to like Diamond, but his wife is a fine woman. I'd have to be sure you didn't mean her any harm before I passed on information of that sort. In these parts, we don't like the sort of men who interfere with womenfolk. See what I mean?'

Barney nodded slowly. 'I appreciate your point of view, but I assure you that my business is with Mrs Diamond, and that I will be acting in her best interests.'

Luker still stayed silent. To pass the time, Barney picked up a tear-off paper pad and started to sketch a likeness of Margaret Pardoe on it. His unconscious efforts had a signal effect upon Luker. He withdrew his objection to giving the information and leaned forward so that he could whisper.

'You ride to the north of town. Follow the old pony express rider's trail till you can line up two tall pines on your left with a highly placed finger of rock, juttin' from an outcrop. Jest past there, turn right in the next stand of timber. After that, keep goin' downhill till you strike the stream. Follow the stream till you find the cabin, half hidden in trees. I still don't know whether I'm doin' the right thing in tellin' you this.'

Luker rose to his feet and stamped

out rather heavily. Barney called his thanks after him, and arranged with the barman to make sure that the stacked coins got into the owner's pocket. He then wandered out into the open, full of speculation about the new slant on things.

★   ★   ★

Around the same time, Dan was standing beside a gnarled tree about a furlong clear of town on the west side. He was smoking and watching the sun go down as he thought of Jenny Braid and the distance between them. He had thankfully given up his oblique enquiries for the evening, and now he was in a semi-comatose state, waiting to muster the energy to go and find his partner.

The creaking wagon which came in a short while later had no special significance for him until a man seated on the box beside the driver called to him by name.

'Hey, Dan! Dan Moore, that is you, ain't it?'

The man who sprang down from the box and came forward to shake his hand was an old acquaintance. A former deputy sheriff, now on leave from his job as a bank security guard.

'Rod,' Dan exclaimed. 'Rod Raven in the flesh. Well what do you know? I never expected to see you in this place. Come to think of it I never expected to be here myself.'

Raven was a tall handsome fellow in his middle thirties with a sprinkling of grey hairs in his dark moustache and sideburns. He talked inconsequentially of this and that, while the older man in charge of the wagon walked round to the tailboard and brought back his riding horse.

Raven accepted the reins, offered money to the man who had given him a ride on account of his mount having picked up a pebble, and bestowed his hearty thanks upon the good-hearted

161

old fellow, who then moved his vehicle nearer town.

'I can guess why you're here, Dan. You're after your old enemy, Kid Diamond. Am I right?'

Dan nodded. He filled his old friend in with a few details of the true position between himself and his enemies and asked what Raven knew about the situation. Raven laid a friendly hand upon his shoulder.

'The position is serious. The Kid is at liberty. Already he has done a robbery and a killin' west of here, an' those peace officers in the know reckon he's headin' this way to contact a saloon keeper in this town who claims to be his brother.'

'Are you sure the Kid did this crime you spoke of?' Dan queried thoughtfully.

'As certain as anyone can be,' Raven returned, 'you see the victim had a thing scratched on his forehead. A knife point had been used to do the job. It was a letter 'K' inside the shape of a diamond. I don't think any lesser criminal would have the nerve to put the Kid's trademark on his handiwork. Do you?'

Dan slowly shook his head. Side by side, the two old friends started back towards the town. Dan felt weighed down by a new responsibility. He would be able to match Barney for news now, but his lucky discovery had not brought with it any enthusiasm for what lay ahead. Rather the opposite.

He wondered how this new knowledge would affect Barney and his latest efforts.

11

Rod Raven went on through the town to spend the night with an acquaintance who lived beyond. Dan found Barney in the room they were to share, patiently waiting and filling in the time by doing physical exercises in his underwear. They had elected to sleep at the Dime.

Dan rolled a couple of smokes and hurriedly started to put his partner in the picture. Ten minutes later, when Barney had also recounted what he had learned, they became silent. Each was thinking out what he intended to do in the near future.

'I'm thinkin' of givin' this character, Johnnie Diamond, protection of a kind,' Dan explained. 'I intend to get out there in front an' keep a watch for the Kid's arrival. After that, I'll play it off the cuff.' He chuckled rather grimly. 'I wouldn't like to be the fellow who pretended to be his brother. Not at this stage in the Kid's career.'

'I expect to ride out to the Diamond shack in the mornin',' Barney murmered, as he rolled his smoke around his lips. 'That bein' so, I could give you some help tonight. I take it you mean to start keepin' watch right away?'

'I do, indeed. That is, after I've talked with the proprietor. He may have some information which would be of use to me. But you don't need to get yourself involved tonight. Take a good sleep. You may be in need of it before the week's out.'

Barney carefully rubbed out his smoke. 'I think I know what you mean. The Kid an' his boys might find out about Mrs Diamond's hideout an' come lookin' for her there. I might even see them before you do.'

'It's a possibility,' Dan admitted, as he catfooted across the floor to the window in his riding boots. 'I hope it doesn't come to that, though. Why don't you get turned in? If the night remains quiet I could give you an early morning call.'

Barney, who looked far from settled and too stimulated to sleep, gave out a hearty yawn. 'All right, amigo. I don't think I'll sleep, but if you say so I'll give it a try.'

Five minutes later, when the young artist was breathing deeply with his eyes closed, Dan blew out the lamp, picked up his rifle and headed out of the bedroom on tiptoe. He had discarded his spurs, but he still feared that he would make a noise and give away his movements.

Earlier in the evening, he had identified the rooms on the front of the building, first floor, where the proprietor and his wife were said to live. Now, he made his way to the first of the rooms, the one which Johnnie Diamond was supposed to sleep in.

He gave a muffled knock, and although no one answered the door a creaking bed frame suggested that the occupant was not asleep. He knocked a second time and sensed the tension he was creating, but again he received no reply.

'Mr Diamond, I've got to talk to you in private. It won't keep until morning.' Dan felt sure his loud whisper was carrying through the keyhole. 'It has to do with the Kid and how soon he gets here. Hurry it up, will you?'

'How do I know you ain't one of the gang tryin' to spring a surprise on me?'

'You don't but I'll come in with my hands raised, if you like. You won't believe it, I'm the fellow who put the Kid away the last time. My name is Dan Moore.'

Johnnie, who so desperately wanted an ally and some protection, took a gamble. He opened the door and drew Dan inside. A lamp hanging from the centre of the ceiling was lit and the two of them sat side by side on the untidy bed.

Diamond provided cigars for them, and presently Dan began to tell what he had so recently heard of the Kid and his latest exploits. Johnnie became more and more restless. From time to time he moved onto his short legs and paced the floor with his hair awry and his quilted dressing gown showing cigar ash.

'Why are you tellin' me all this, deputy? I know I'm in danger an' I have to keep my nerve. All you're doin' is wearin' me down. I'll be in a poor state when I have to face up to the Kid. I know he'll be after me for pretendin' to be his brother an' all that. But, well, what am I goin' to do?'

'You're goin' to keep your nerve an' act as a decoy, so that I can get close to the Kid without him bein' aware of it. Will you help?'

The saloon keeper looked up briefly and wrung his hands. He peered all around the room as if the bathroom or the second bedroom might secretly contain enemies. Finally his troubled eyes came back to regard Dan.

'My nerves are shot already. I thought I heard somebody tiptoein' along to this suite a half hour before you knocked. It ain't goin' to be easy for me. What is it you want me to do?'

'Jest carry on as if you hadn't seen me. If the Kid comes try an' pacify him. Play for time. Keep him calm. I promise you that if I get a chance with him he won't do you any serious harm. I'm goin' to keep watch from that two-storey buildin' across the street. Know the one I mean?'

Johnnie nodded without enthusiasm. 'Sure, that's the old dentist's house. There's no ceiling in it between the ground floor and the old bedrooms, because there was a fire an' the inner shell was burnt out. Do you have to go that far away?'

Dan grinned in the light of the lamp. He was trying to give poor 'Diamond' a bit of confidence to see him through the night. He said several things, but when he left the apartment, he felt that Johnnie was as nervous as when he first saw him.

Armed with a cold meat pie from the

Dime's kitchen, he slipped inconspicuously across the street and eased his way into the building. For three or four minutes his eyes were not properly adjusted to the gloom. After that, however, he gained confidence and set about setting himself up to watch.

★   ★   ★

The first intimation that Johnnie Diamond had that all was not well was when he saw the strip of light showing under the door which communicated with the second bedroom. He was stretched out on the bed, sucking spasmodically at a second cigar, when he became aware of the light. The weed fell from his lips and he had to chase it fumblingly across the bedding to avoid setting himself on fire. Having retrieved it, he cleard his throat and tried to dismiss from his mind his deepest fears.

'Who's that in there?'

His voice started out on a firm note, but faded before he had completed the question. A man chuckled, but the sound was so quiet that he did not know what to make of it. The utterance had confirmed that someone was indeed in the other room, but who it was, and for what purpose he had no idea.

He was about to shout a second time when the door opened towards him and a stranger moved in upon him carrying the lamp. Johnnie sat up with a jerk and gave out with a noise like the gasp of a half-strangled person.

'*Stay where you are and keep quiet, brother!*'

'You are the Kid? Truly?'

The Kid put down the lamp on a narrow table set against the wall, near the door. His shadow bulked to twice his normal size as he crouched close and turned down the wick to the lowest level without its going out.

'Sure, I'm the Kid. Ain't you pleased to see me? A man ought to get a special welcome from his kin, especially when he's fresh out of the territorial penitentiary. So why don't you act friendly?'

Kid Diamond was thirty-six years old; tall, handsome and dominating. In the indefinite light of the lamp his wide mouth looked even wider. His dark bright eyes looked like grey bullet tips. A cut on his left upper eyelid had healed so that it gave the same effect as a hare lip.

A recently grown brown moustache adorned his upper lip, breaking the rather flat contours of his unusual face. The Kid came a little closer and held out a hand, which gave an enormous shadow that reached out towards the terrified man. Johnnie never knew how he refrained in that instant from crying for help. The Kid lifted the small table to the side of the bed without upsetting the lamp.

As he did so, his pseudo brother got a clear glimpse of the diamond with the 'K' inside it, tattooed on the back of his left hand. Johnnie really began to think then that he would not survive the night.

What was it the deputy had said?

Play for time. Play for time! How could a man in the last extremities of fear will himself into playing for time? He cautiously put his legs over the side of the bed and turned sideways.

'It was a stupid thing for me to do, makin' out I was your brother, Kid. I hope you ain't riled by what I've done. Maybe I can help you? You wouldn't have slipped into this apartment at dead of night if you didn't need help. What can I do for you?'

The Kid eyed him critically. He helped himself to a cigar from the drawer of the table and lit it with a match from the same place.

'Who was that fellow you were talkin' to in here a short while back?'

'Him? Oh, nobody compared with you, Kid. A boaster, he was. Some hombre who claimed to have put you in prison. Come to think of it, he didn't look like a peace officer to me.'

Johnnie was just beginning to feel the slightest bit more at ease when his unwanted visitor grabbed him by the neck of his night attire and so twisted the cloth that he almost choked.

'Describe him! Think, you fool. What did he look like?'

This was an exercise at which Johnnie Dimes was not very good. Nevertheless, he made a brave attempt to give the information required. He reasoned that while he was allowed to talk he would not be in danger of strangulation.

'He was maybe twenty-six or twenty-eight years old. His hair was dark an' long down the sides of his face. I couldn't see the colour of his eyes, but they looked kind of intense. You know what I mean? And his name was Dan something.'

'Dan Moore!' the Kid breathed, in a deep scarcely-controlled voice.

'Yer, that's it, Kid. Dan Moore. So he was tellin' the truth when he said he was a deputy?'

Actually Dan had never claimed to be a deputy, Johnnie had assumed it. The Kid's eyes were weaving this way and that as he mulled over this timely piece of information. So Dan Moore had nibbled at the bait, leaving Conchas Creek behind and coming out to look for the Kid of his own initiative. Moreover, he was looking in the right place.

The Kid moved to Johnnie's side again. 'Where is he now?'

A wavering stubby finger pointed to the window. 'He's across there, keepin' watch for you in that two-storey buildin'. He's a wily bird, all right, Kid, but he's no match for you. What are you goin' to do about him?'

The outlaw drew his index finger across his throat and made a certain sound. The saloon-keeper gasped and his tormentor chuckled.

'Anybody else keepin' watch?'

'Not that I know of. I never saw that deputy before tonight. I wouldn't know what he has in mind, other than to keep watch over there, like he said.'

'Do you have any money in this apartment?' the Kid queried suddenly.

A faint spark of courage flickered in the oppressed man at the mention of money. He managed a chuckle of sorts. 'No, Kid, I never keep any up here. Why, anybody might walk in an' help themselves, eh? There's maybe fifty bucks in the safe down below, in my office. Otherwise I keep the takings in the bank down the street. We have to be businesslike these days.'

The Kid nodded. When he moved, he did so with startling speed. His fist caught Johnnie in the neck and sent him breathless and sprawling back on the bed. The outlaw followed up and his face was within two inches of the other's as Johnnie gasped for breath.

'Think again, big brother. Make me think you're a generous relation. You ought to be takin' me seriously by now.'

The Kid did not believe him and he had been caught out in a lie. He trailed a hand and arm towards the table at the side of the bed. The ex-convict backed away a foot or two, and patiently awaited the next development. Johnnie fumbled around the side of the table. His index finger tip encountered a button which released a small, secret drawer in the side. The outlaw then brushed him aside and helped himself to the wad of notes hidden there. He did not know at the time, but they amounted to about two hundred and fifty dollars.

'Johnnie, you've annoyed me jest now. An' I ain't the sort to take this kind of treatment in the middle of the night. So what do we do? First of all, we turn out the lamp, in case that peepin' peace officer over there gets the idea of takin' a look over here. I want to do the visitin'. I'd prefer for him to stay there for a while.'

Feeling safe in the presence of his cowed prisoner, the Kid blew out the lamp and went silently over towards the window, wrinkling his nostrils at the smell put up by the extinguished wick. While he was standing there in the shadowy gloom, Johnnie summoned all his courage for one piece of hostile action.

He hauled himself up a few inches and reached under the head of the bed for the revolver which hung in its holster there. His groping hand disturbed the gun belt, but located the gun. He drew it and was hauling it through the metal bars of the bed head when a slight clink of metal warned the man at the window.

The Kid sprang about. His right hand swept down to waist level, came up rather swiftly to his shoulder and then released his weapon. The knife, hastily aimed because of the darkness and the need for speed, nevertheless was on target. The point of it penetrated between two of Johnnie's ribs and entered the heart.

Life started to ebb out of him at once. He appeared to shrivel and to collapse back on the bed. His gun hand spilled over the side and the heavy weapon dropped from his powerless fingers. The Kid licked his lips in the dark, holding back for a few moments as though he was waiting for an echo.

Presently, he crossed to the bed and made the mark of the 'K' and the diamond on the back of Johnnie's hand. It pleased him to do it by touch, in the dark. He stayed by the bed for perhaps a minute before his interest dwindled. Then he went back to the window.

12

The Kid remained by the window breathing hard for more than five minutes. In that time he absently cleaned the blade of his knife on the dead man's curtains. His thoughts travelled from his disposal of the saloon keeper to the coming clash with his old enemy, Dan Moore.

Diamond had not thought to settle the issue so soon after his release from the penitentiary, but here, in the small town of Ford, and because of his forethought, the deputy was giving him an opportunity to settle the matter straight away.

The silent man smiled to himself in the dark. What a sensation his ruthless exploits of this night would cause when the townsfolk of Ford learned the truth about the night's happenings. The first saloon keeper of the town dead, in his own bed, and also a deputy who had been fully alert to the possible dangers.

The Kid had his gang not far from town. He could call upon them at a few hour's notice, but that did not appear to be necessary. They knew he had sworn to kill Moore, and it was far better from the Kid's point of view that the deputy should be killed without the assistance of others.

In the eyes of the general public, the Kid's image would be blown up considerably, so that he presented a much greater menace than he had ever done before his capture. Given time, songs might very well be written about him.

The movement of a cat down the street drew his attention and reminded him that the night would not last forever. He had to make plans. Any sort of delay in a situation like this one could only lead to unnecessary risk, and that was something he could do without. He was quite sure that Dan was where Johnnie Diamond had said he was, and that Dan had sufficient patience to watch all through the night. Nevertheless, it might be a good thing to start moving.

If Moore was to be surprised at his vigil, the empty building he was using would have to be approached stealthily. And from the front. The Kid did not have the patience to investigate the rear of the building.

In order to achieve his aim, he had to slip out of the Dime building into the street and make his way to the other place either from one side or the other. Which way would be best?

He shifted back to the bed, lit a match and studied the corpse and other items. When the match stick flickered out he was ready to collect his own gear, and one or two small items of Johnnie's and make his exit.

No one challenged him in the corridor outside. He slipped down the staircase like a ghost, pausing in the rear of the big drinking and gaming room below. As always in wooden buildings, a board creaked here and there, but he made nothing of it.

He crossed to the bar, brought up a whiskey bottle from the rear of it and gave himself a good drink from the neck. Caution, and the need for a clear head made him stop drinking before he had had his fill. He placed the bottle down rather carefully on the scarred bar counter and promised himself that he would come back and finish it off, if all went according to plan.

Next, he moved towards the front entrance, where the swinging batwings moved almost imperceptibly in the night breeze. He could slide out that way, but if he did so, he might reveal his presence to the sharp-eyed deputy who was keeping a vigil simply to apprehend him.

Shrugging unseen, the outlaw backed away, and retired to the back of the room, seeking a way out at the rear.

* * *

About the same time, Dan Moore, perched on his ladder at the upper front window of the deserted house, got a craving to smoke. His tired eyes took in both aspects of the street once again. The entire lack of movement, or of incident assured him that he could relax for a minute or two and indulge himself in the pleasures of nicotine.

He glanced down the ladder. His hat and a leather vest were hanging around the top end of a wooden plank, some five feet above the ground. The vest he had brought along in case the night vigil proved a cold one. The hat he had discarded because it helped to make him too comfortable, and comfort in the night meant drowsiness.

The plank was propped against the lower part of the ladder to give a little extra support, and the makings were in a pocket of the vest. In order to get them, he had to come down several rungs and grope about with one hand. The tobacco sack came out of the pocket fairly easily. Extracting the matches from his hat band took a little more time, but presently he had what he wanted and he went back up to his second storey window.

He turned his back on the street for a short while and sat on the top rung with his legs bent and his heels on a lower one. Presently, his intake of smoke, scarcely visible in the gloom, afforded him a slight sense of contentment. The possibility that the Kid might turn up at any time seemed very remote. When he thought about it, Dan envied Barney a comfortable bed in the hotel.

Even Johnnie Diamond was in comfort, although he was fearful.

* * *

A whole half hour elapsed before the Kid began to make his way down the other side of the street, heading cautiously for the lookout building. As he came nearer, he deliberately slowed. Nothing was going to forewarn the watcher and give him a chance to get the upper hand.

A Kid Diamond killing was a thorough one. Nothing was going to interfere with this one. The feeling was born out of revenge for the countless months spent in a hostile building, taking orders from bullying guards and eating inferior food. Dan Moore was going to get his. The end would have to come quickly, but surely the deputy would have a few seconds in which he knew who it was who had found his hideout and beaten him at his own game?

The Kid hoped so. He shook with fervour as he negotiated the front of the building directly beyond the deputy's hideout. In order to cross the front of this one without giving away his presence, he went down on his knees, beyond the end of the sidewalk, and pressed his body against the front boards. Foot by foot, he moved on.

Flaking paint adhered to his clothing. A thin splinter of wood entered the back of his hand where the special identifying mark was tattooed. He felt the pain, but refused to let it deter him. He removed his conspicuous straw hat and came at last to the final alleyway.

There, he laid himself down in the dust and contemplated the vital building through half-closed eyes. He marvelled at the patience which his adversary must have to spend the night in such a derelict spot with little to charm away the hours, or to give him comfort.

After that, the approach was at its most difficult. He negotiated the slight gap across the alley by wriggling along almost like a newt. Once started upon this stretch there was no stopping. As he inched forward, he saw that the glass was still intact in the windows of both levels. His straining eyes suggested that there was something other than ordinary shadow behind both windows, but he allowed nothing to dissuade him from his task.

The whole of his muscular body was covered in light perspiration by the time he had crossed under the lower window and reached the step of the front door.

And there he rested. He had to be in good form for his surprise entry. Any sort of slip up at this stage could only end in disaster.

He discarded his hat, leaving it on the ground. He made sure that his knife was loose-fitting in its sheath and then he turned his attention to his matched twin .44s. This was an action when guns had to be used. In the dark, a knife could miss its mark, and that was always a bad moment for the thrower. His guns would avail him of twelve shots in a short space of time. Enough lethal lead to kill a man who had been out of target on entry. Enough shells to spray the whole room, in the dark. He hoped that it would not be absolutely necessary to empty both guns, but he was prepared for such an eventuality.

The base of the door moved a fraction in response to his probing finger. He felt sure that it would open altogether, provided he gave it a firm push. Now, he was almost ready for the assault. He paused, however, and glanced up at the windows of Johnnie Diamond's private quarters on the other side of the street.

The Kid was telling himself that he had achieved much already that evening by stealth. Now, he was about to break the night stillness and give Ford the greatest shock of its history. Moving quite quietly, he came to his knees.

So far as he could tell there was no responsive reaction from the windows, but he did not wait to confirm such a thing. Kicking open the door, he sprang through it, rolling forward in a rather spectacular acrobatic manoeuvre which was really a somersault with hands and arms clear of the floor.

In making this move, he knew that he was taking a chance, not knowing if any article of furniture stood there in the dark to bar his way and to damage him. Fortunately, the space ahead of him was bare. The back of his shoulders connected with the floor boards. He rolled into an upright position, sprang about and did one of his fast gun draws.

The front wall of the house was in inky black shadow. From somewhere on that side, a startled gasp went up. Blinking sharply against the intensified gloom, the Kid brought up his weapons and spent a mere second or two in seeking his target. His sharp eyes picked out the silhouette of a stetson and that was enough for him.

He blasted off with both guns a foot beneath the level of the hat and at the same time slowly moved sideways. The room was filled with a succession of gun flashes. Gun smoke piled up in the dusty atmosphere, entirely killing the earlier odour of tobacco smoke.

The succession of bullets continued. The hat flew off and dropped to one side. Likewise an article of clothing. Wood splinters flew here and there, and when most of the rounds had been fired, a most unexpected thing occurred; something which the Kid could never have allowed for.

Hidden in that thick gloom was a long ladder. His shells ripped into it, all at the same level, and suddenly it parted. The upper half was precipitated to the floor and with it came the sound of a body falling hard. Diamond had expected Moore to slump, but not a heavy fall from on high.

To heighten the brief but unbearable tension in the ambush room, a shoulder weapon bounced on the floorboards and discharged itself. The bigger bullet flew in the Kid's direction and thoroughly startled him. He crouched and darted even further to his right, withholding one round in each gun and peering with great intensity into the gloom as he searched for the body of his fallen enemy.

Before he identified the true spot, another six-gun began to fire back at him. If the deputy was wounded, or injured by the fall, he was still active enough to retaliate. The Kid fired his remaining rounds at the same time as Moore rolled to one side.

There was a second when no one moved, and then the Kid made a sudden dart and a dive for a window located in the rear wall of the room. He went through it in a neat dive, taking glass with him, and closely followed up by two hostile bullets which were within inches of wounding him. Once through the window, the Kid dived through a low over-dry hedge and came to his feet as he rounded an angle of the building and crossed open ground at the rear.

Dan Moore also used the window, but he was moving more slowly, exhibiting more caution, and doing nothing to aggravate any strains he might have received during his precipitate fall from the top of the ladder.

The Kid's retiring footsteps quickly faded away. Dan propped himself against a side wall of the house. He was thankful to have survived so dastardly an attack, but he could not help thinking that he had been thoroughly outmanoeuvred by his old enemy, and that knowledge rather undermined his confidence.

After making a circuit of the building, he returned to the front door. He was examining the Kid's straw hat when tense and nervous townsmen appeared and demanded to know who he was and what his business was. The local peace officer pushed his way through the small crowd and Dan presented him with the discarded hat.

'Good mornin', marshal,' he began calmly. 'I'm from Conchas Creek. Deputy Dan Moore. I have to tell you that Kid Diamond visited your town tonight, and he very nearly blasted me to kingdom come in this empty building. I'd be glad if you'd accompany me to the Dime establishment, because the Kid came here really to take his revenge upon Johnnie Diamond for pretendin' to be his brother.'

The veteran marshal, one of two brothers who ramrodded the town, took a little time to digest the proffered information. After asking a couple of questions, Jake Hawke pronounced himself ready to go along with the stranger's suggestions. A livery man stopped them as they reached the swing doors of the Dime. He informed the peace officers that a stranger had entered his place a few minutes ago and left in a hurry on a palomino horse.

'That would be the Kid gettin' clear of town,' Dan surmised.

Marshal Hawke massaged his white moustache, glanced at his brother who had just joined them and headed the trio into the building. Inevitably they found the corpse of the proprietor. Dan fed them some details of the Diamond Kid and his recent exploits. His own threatening letter merited some interest, too.

Jake and Mark Hawke, who could muster one hundred and ten summers between them, seemed a trifle nonplussed by this sudden serious crime in the middle of the night. Dan noted this. He excused himself and went back to his own room to satisfy his curiosity about Barney. He had half expected his partner to show up when the gun shots reverberated around the town.

Barney had already gone. He had tried to sleep, but failed, and not very long after Dan had left he had scribbled a note to say that he was too restless for sleep. He had packed his few belongings and moved out of town on horseback. His intention had been to ride up the track towards the north and sleep for a few hours in the open.

Dan began to pace the room. He said aloud. 'Well, amigo, I hope you make out better than I did.'

He was still pacing when the Hawke brothers came along to have further talk with him.

13

The penetrating heat of the day was just beginning to build up that following morning when Barney Malone looked down from the crest of a hill slope and saw for the first time the location of Margaret Pardoe Diamond's out-of-town retreat.

The lush foliage of the trees round about him were swaying in a slight breeze which fanned both horse and rider and gave them a feeling of well-being. Barney, however, did not trust this excessive calm. He knew that trouble was on the way and that it might have already arrived.

There was a thin plume of smoke coming from the chimney of the timber house half hidden in its own small copse; proof enough that someone was in occupation. Barney had no reason to suppose that it had been kindled by anyone other than the women he sought. He dismounted and rocked his saddle, wondering as he did so about the mental attitude of a woman who could desire this sort of life, away from fellow humans and the amenities of towns.

He was more than a little curious about Mrs Pardoe. Obviously she had brains, education and some culture, otherwise she would not have appealed to men as different as Johnnie Diamond and Victor Pardoe. He wondered if she had regrets about her course of action in leaving the doctor, and if so, whether she managed to live with them and stay happy.

Barney rolled himself a smoke. He walked about while the big dappled animal cropped grass and generally relaxed after a ride of two hours. Through a newly acquired spyglass he studied the distant dwelling and saw much to interest him. It had a splendid chimney, centrally placed in the roof and built of stone. He wondered if there was an ordinary everyday stove pipe leading into it, or whether Johnnie Diamond had planned something more elaborate and expensive. The well-painted green window shutters and the window drapes also took his attention.

Nothing occurred to disturb him, but a growing feeling of unease persisted, and for a minute or more, he wondered what it was about. Eventually, he decided that it was because he could not see any sign of human movement. He felt that Margaret ought to be out and about, doing her chores, and yet she was nowhere in evidence.

He rubbed out the butt of his smoke and wondered how he could find out more without actually showing himself at the house. The sound of running water prompted his thoughts in a new direction. The stream was some two hundred yards away towards his left, on lower ground.

If he approached along the lower ground favoured by the watercourse he stood a far better chance of getting closer unnoticed. Having decided upon this course of action, he implemented it at once, and some ten minutes later he had paused again, once more hidden by the foliage of a tree. This time it was a willow, the slender, pliant branches of which hung wide of the bank and almost touched the bubbling surface of the stream.

Below him, the stream took a turn to the left and broadened out quite unexpectedly. He guessed that it was between three and five feet deep and he could see at once that Margaret Pardoe made good use of it. She was in there, and apparently naked, taking a mid-morning bathe in the modest shelter of the hanging foliage on the far side of the bathing spot.

Barney whistled quietly to himself as he watched her. She swam with a slow graceful breast-stroke which revealed and hid her shapely neck and shoulders. Even at that distance, he could detect the features which he had reproduced from Victor Pardoe's photographs. Her long black hair hung around her face and neck like a tightly-fitting cowl. Although the trees shadowed her, as a subject for a drawing the swimmer took Barney's breath away.

He watched through his glass and felt like an eavesdropper, a Peeping Tom. And he was just that, he supposed. His cheeks burned as he thought about it. He became restless. Just as his conscience was winning a battle to have the observation stopped, he detected something which seemed a little out of touch with the general scene.

Clinging to hanging vegetation, the young woman turned and stared across the water towards the further bank, which was out of sight to the observer. There was something in her expression which suggested that she was not completely at ease; that something else was there to disturb her.

Again, Barney thought of shifting his position. This time he dismounted and found a scrub oak which was readily climbable. He discarded his spurs and climbed it without undue effort. The increased altitude at once paid off. Through his glass he could clearly see the cause of Margaret's discomfiture.

She was observed by two men. One was about fifty yards back, directly across from her bathing spot, and the other was further upstream on the same side as his partner, but nearer the bank. The one in the closer position had a broad face and a fair beard, while the other one was tall and broad, dressed in a black outfit, and seemingly having a countenance both pale and expressionless.

At once, Barney began to tense up. He measured the distance between the watchers and the bathing woman with his eyes, and decided that they must be showing some sort of respect for her. Clearly, Margaret had crossed the water by a low wooden bridge now visible slightly nearer than the bathing spot. She had probably crossed it on foot and undressed on the far side, away from her male escort.

Both the two men had an edgy furtive way of moving; it was as though they were accustomed to being on the watch for enemies. Barney dubbed them at once as outlaws, although he had little experience with such people. He surmised quite correctly that he was seeing members of the Kid Diamond gang, and this conclusion gave him no peace of mind.

If the gang were in touch with Mrs 'Diamond' it could only mean trouble for her, or for her husband; probably for both.

Barney shared his attention between the two restless observers and the bather, who was obviously getting ready to leave the water. Again, he had a feeling that the men had some respect for the woman. Those who would have interfered with her would have been located a good deal closer.

At least in this respect, the outlaws appeared to be keeping the code of the west, the unspoken rule that westerners did not interfere with women in isolated places.

Barney caught a glimpse of Margaret as she rose a few inches clear of the surface and waded out under the trees. An impression of her shape impinged upon his artist's memory before the shadowed area under the foliage blotted her out. Barney swallowed hard and sighed. He glanced down the tree below him and wondered what he should do.

No one clattered across the bridge to interfere with the privacy of the woman, and there was nothing to make Barney suppose that she was in any immediate personal danger. He tried to plan something, and he decided that he might be in the best position to make contact with her if he hurried to the empty house and secreted himself there before she returned.

★ ★ ★

The backtracking detour which he had to make at speed and without any revealing noise brought him out in a coat of perspiration before five minutes had gone by. Soon, he was taking the grey down the gentle slope to the house itself.

His drawing board, normally strapped to his back, remained at the foot of his lookout tree. He hoped that he would survive what lay ahead and that he would be able to retrieve it when this business of Margaret Pardoe and her 'followers' was all cleared up and resolved.

Fifty yards short of the house, he thought he heard a sound coming from within. He slowed the sweating grey and became very watchful. Just when he thought he had company, someone he had not accounted for, a grey squirrel bounded across the roof and leapt for a widely-spread tree branch. Barney saw it, relaxed a little and sighed.

He searched for a place to hide his horse and found one some fifty yards away where a tree had once been uprooted in a storm. He loosened the saddle, put the animal on a long tethering rope and hurried to the house with his long curling neck hairs prickling. So far, no one had appeared from the timber directly above the bathing spot, but they could show up at any time. Fortune favoured him, however, and he was able to gain the shelter of the house without being seen by anyone who was also approaching.

Just inside the door, he paused, pulled off his hat and ruffled his long thick hair. His eyes were busy as he worked to recover his breath. Inside, the walls had been smoothed, and here and there stylish paintings of French origin graced the blank spaces.

In the first room, a fine three-piece suite of dark leather was tastefully arranged. The fireplace was a round one, exactly in the centre of the room and the chimney above it opened out to take the smoke like the mouth of a blunderbuss. There was a gap all the way round between the fireplace and the chimney to allow the heat to get out and for cooking to be done on two horizontal metal plates.

The main room occupied half of the floor. The rest of the ground floor area was partitioned off. The other part was partitioned again into a kitchen and a bedroom. Barney took time out to glance into both. He noted the expensive drapes on the high, double bed, and a tall wardrobe built as a fixture against the far wall.

Hastily he backed out, and wondered where he should be when the owner of the house arrived. He had to assume that the outlaws would come in with her, and that meant concealment, or a show of force with weapons before he had the chance to speak to Margaret in private.

His questing eyes noted the loft over the kitchen and bedroom. A neat ladder some eight feet in length was resting horizontally along the foot of a wall. Already, his ears had detected the sound of a horse coming into the vicinity of the house from the direction of the stream. He was in a hurry to get out of sight and the loft seemed to present the best place. If he had to make his presence known in a hurry, the upper level offered the best opportunity of taking the undesirable males by surprise.

He clambered to the top and leaned down again. By hooking a foot behind a rung of the ladder he was able to drop it without too much noise back in the place where he had found it. He turned his attention to the loft. Built in cupboards, shaped to the slope of the roof, occupied the extremities on either side. Two or three bottles of perfume stood on a narrow kidney shaped cabinet near one of the twin low-framed camp-style beds and this made Barney think that Margaret did not always sleep down below in splendid isolation.

The steady approach of a lightly-built riding horse made Barney shuffle around. He decided to hide himself on the sheepskin rug which softened the boards between the twin beds. He lowered himself upon it and took his ease, removing his hat and placing his .45 beside him.

He was as ready for the meeting as he would ever be, but he could not help thinking that Dan Moore would have done better in his place for what was to follow.

★   ★   ★

Margaret Pardoe Diamond dismounted from her small pinto mare, unsaddling it with a slight show of haste, and dumping the gear without ceremony outside the front door of the house on the way in.

She was breathless and not a little put out by the situation which had been thrust upon her the previous day. In taking her daily bathe in the stream, she had been trying out her captors to see if they would permit her to go out of sight. They had not, of course, but they had not attempted to molest her and she supposed that that was something to be thankful for.

She spread her towel on a rail hanging from the bell-like chimney and removed the soft grey felt flat-crowned hat which had hidden her hair. She licked her neatly shaped small lips with the tip of her tongue as she peered through a window and wondered if the intruders were coming in after her.

She saw them slowly approach, riding casually and full of confidence. The man with the flat deadpan expression was apparently talking. He must have said something funny, a rare happening, because the man referred to as McGillie began to laugh in a way which rocked his fleshy frame in the saddle.

They kept glancing towards the house, but they were in no hurry to come in; for which Margaret was thankful. It needed all her dignity for her not to break down in their presence. Now, when it seemed that she had a minute or two to herself, she tried to relax.

When she was out in the wilds, she wore men's clothing. Today she had on a man's shirt patterned with black and red squares, and a pair of expensive denims fringed with leather like a cowpuncher's chaps.

Her nervous fingers undid the top buttons of the shirt. She sighed and glanced at herself in a rectangular mirror flat against one wall. A stranger might have thought that she was still nearer twenty than thirty, were it not for the unbecoming dark smudges underneath her eyes; marks which had appeared since the arrival of the outlaws.

Her shoulders shook with a sob or two, but she held on and began to comb out her long tresses with a curved comb bearing silver teeth.

'Oh hell, Johnnie Diamond, why don't you come out here an' put an end to this unfair situation?'

Her voice was low and vibrant. Barney was moved by it, but he felt that he could not afford to waste any time, in case the two men decided to come indoors before he had made himself known.

He cleared his throat. Still out of sight from him, Margaret trembled and moved swiftly towards a long narrow table. Her hands were on the fitted drawer when Barney spoke out.

'I'm sorry I had to come into your house without warning, Mrs Diamond, but I could see earlier that you had unwelcome visitors. My name is Barney Malone, an' I've come here on behalf of your husband. Naturally, as you are in trouble I'll do anything I can to help you. Is it all right to show myself now?'

'Yes. Yes, of course get down out of that loft, an' hurry. But no, wouldn't it be better if you stayed there, in case we're taken by surprise? Tell me, is Johnnie intendin' to come out this way? Does he have any idea what's goin' on?'

Margaret came away from the drawer and the weapon she kept in it. Barney, meanwhile, showed his head out of the loft.

'Johnnie Diamond may well come out this way to see what's happenin' to you, ma'am, but I meant your real

211

husband, Victor Pardoe. Surely you haven't forgotten him altogether?'

Barney's sincere blue eyes suddenly looked less clear because Margaret's own had filled up with tears. She dropped her gaze, and her shoulders shook. The intruder was a little surprised himself. He wanted to go down there and comfort her, but the close proximity of danger prevented him from doing so.

He straightened up in the loft, and thoughtfully wondered how the imminent clash with the outlaws would turn out.

14

'Margaret, if you feel so deeply about Vic Pardoe why haven't you gone back to him before now?'

The woman blew her nose and made an effort to stifle her emotions for both their sakes. 'How can you ask me to go back to Pardoe after the way I treated him? You did come here to ask me to return to him, didn't you? I ran away an' left him, don't you understand? And now I'm mixed up in something connected with my man, Johnnie Diamond.

'I don't want you to ask me why I stay with a man like Johnnie. He attracted me once, an' he still likes to have me around. Besides, he may be tricky an' act rough at times but he's kind. If he cheats other people, he doesn't cheat me, an' that's a fact. But what do we do now?

213

'You've blundered in at a time when we have other problems. As soon as the outlaws get to know you're on my side an' not theirs, your life won't be worth a plugged nickel. My advice to you is to get out while you still have a chance. I can say you were a thief, or something.'

Barney ignored the advice. He stayed on the alert, however, and was pleased when Margaret started to move around the room in an ordinary everyday manner. 'Tell me about the outlaws,' he murmured.

Margaret made sure the coffee pot was securely placed on the fire before answering. 'There's two of them here. So far the famous Kid has not shown up. Judgin' by hints dropped by these two he's in town an' seekin' to contact Johnnie direct. They also mention another partner of theirs. A man with a French-sounding name. They refer to him now and again as the Corsican. He seems to be overdue. More than that I can't tell you, except about the two men who have latched onto me. The tall one is called Tom. Nevada Tom. He's tall and around forty, I'd say. He has these peculiar eyes which I can only think reflect his particular kind of ruthlessness. He has a lot of crisp dark hair, and he always dresses in black.'

Margaret shuddered briefly as she tended the frying pan.

'Men who wear black always make me think of funerals and death. Maybe that's why they do it. The other man is shorter and heavier, but I'd swear he's just as deadly. Bruce McGillie. He has a fair beard, and I'd wager his great head is round because his black hat is that shape. It's flat on top, too. Not that that signifies anything, but he is bald up from his forehead.

'If they have anything in common it's restless arms. I get the impression they spend half their lives straining towards their guns, but maybe I'm wrong. So that's what they're like. This far they've held themselves in check and not been too objectionable. They're waiting for the Kid, and they seem to be a little bit wary of him.

'So, as I said before, what are we goin' to do? Are you goin' to try an' jump the pair of them, or what?'

The young woman stood with her hands on her hips and stared up at Barney. She was obviously very interested in him and his brand of courage. He, for his part, was already outlining her on a sheet of paper in his mind. He found himself doing this mental exercise, in spite of their predicament.

'I guess I'll jest have to play it as it comes,' he said, after a short pause. 'I can't jest slip away. After all, Mr Pardoe paid me a retainer of sorts, an' I'm sure he'd want me to do what I can for his beloved wife. Tell me this, if I manage to get you out of the clutches of these outlaws, will you come back with me to Conchas Creek?'

The fleeting emotions tormenting the frightened young woman showed in her face. Any sort of a decision at that time was beyond her. She sounded very cross when she answered him.

'Oh, how I hate men sometimes! How can you think of making bargains at a time like this? If you were a religious person you'd spend this time in prayin' for deliverance, not tryin' to extract promises from strange women whose affairs you don't understand!'

Just as Barney was about to reply angrily, a man laughed rather coarsely not far from the house. This had a signal effect upon the two people already in it. Barney ducked out of sight, and Margaret bent over the fire and put more bacon in the pan. For a few seconds, the only sounds in the house were made by the fire and the bubbling coffee pot.

Nevada was the one who threw open the door. He studied Margaret every bit as closely as Barney might have done, but the look in his eyes suggested a different type of interest. McGillie brushed past his friend and moved around the main room as though suspicious about something.

His eyes went to the drying towel and

then to Margaret's body. He looked as if he regretted not having gone in for a swim with her. Now, the bearded man was hoping that the Kid would not come for a day or two. This house was comfortable and restful, and at another time it might be possible to bathe with this rather unusual, beautiful but withdrawn woman.

Nevada also watched her, but she did not respond and he helped himself to the coffee pot and poured out for two. When he had sipped coffee, he asked in a low voice if Margaret had enjoyed her swim. He received no answer. To cover his disappointment and loss of face Nevada started to laugh.

'You wait till the Kid gets here. Women always talk for him, Mrs Diamond. I figure you're goin' to really like your brother-in-law.' He paused for a moment and scratched his head. His eyes were on McGillie when he resumed. 'I suppose she's still the Kid's sister-in-law, even if Johnnie's dead? Ain't that so?'

The woman turned pale, but held on to her control with an effort. McGillie sampled the coffee, swirled it around his mouth, and shrugged his heavy shoulders.

'I couldn't rightly say, Tom, but one way or the other, it won't trouble the Kid. You know him. So how long is that meal goin' to take? Watchin' females swimmin' always gives me an appetite.'

Margaret blushed, and the two men laughed. They were still laughing when another sound came to them from the bedroom. It was a peculiar noise which affected Mrs Diamond and the man hidden in her loft far more than the other two. It was the sound of high-pitched, almost soundless laughter. Nevada and McGillie had heard it before because they reacted at once, sharing their surprise but being in no way disturbed.

There was a creaking noise which was caused by the door of the built-in wardobe being forced open to its maximum. The small man who moved silently on short legs into the presence of the others caused a minor sensation.

Nevada stabbed a long index finger in his direction. 'The Corsican was in here ahead of us!'

'Yer, Ludeau's been holdin' out on us,' McGillie added. 'How long have you been hidin' in that wardrobe, Pierre?'

Margaret Diamond seemed rooted to the spot. She just had to know how long this rather sinister figure had been in her house. Her frightened eyes checked over his appearance. He was about thirty-five years of age, and below the average in height. He was broad and particularly thick through the chest. His legs were short and his arms over-long. He walked with a muscular apelike roll. His dark hair was sheared close to his skull, but a sprinkling of silver hairs still showed.

He blinked his heavy, bulbous eyes several times very slowly as he stared at the woman.

'I've been there long enough to know

that all you've said since you came in has been overheard, an' I don't mean only by the woman, either.'

He glanced briefly at his friends, set his weight evenly between his two feet and patted his chest, which at that time was encompassed by a plaid coat. He was just in the act of turning around when Barney's body hurtled out of the loft and the free-for-all started.

Margaret screamed. The young artist headed like a diver over water for Nevada, the man he took to be the greatest menace. If he had thought longer, Barney might have tried to get the drop on all three from above, but the Corsican's sudden revelation had spoiled his calculations. On the way down, the young man's shoulder caught the side of the fireplace surround. That was unfortunate, because he winced with pain and lost his revolver, even as he connected with the tall man in the dark outfit. Nevada went over backwards.

McGillie made an effort to get clear

of entanglement and keep that way. Unfortunately, due to the general excitement he collided with the loft ladder and knocked it sideways, spoiling himself for an early gun shot as Barney and Nevada rolled across the floor on the other side of the fireplace.

The Corsican was the one who really kept out of trouble. He retreated as far as the door by which he had entered and his muscular body was ready for anything. He hovered there, his hands above his waist belt, ready to move in or to draw his guns.

Barney broke clear. He dived after his gun, but Nevada managed to drop a foot on his wrist before he could grab it and fire. Barney retaliated by rolling into the leg which pinioned him. Nevada lost his balance again and struck the side of his head on the fireplace. He lost his hat and was partially stunned.

In the meantime, McGillie, who was not keen on this type of indoor fighting, sought to put an end to it. He grabbed for Margaret, intending to use her as a shield and as a target to dissuade Barney from further action. The young woman failed to slip his clutching hand, but she wriggled to such good effect that the bearded man had to pivot on his heels. She gripped his wrist and his reflex action had the effect of firing off his weapon.

The discharge of the gun in the enclosed space had a signal effect upon everyone in the house. The Corsican was still rocking on his heels and toes, but this time his motion was in a different direction. Margaret, coughing upon the smoke of the weapon discharged so close to her, stared at the small sinister figure with her hands lightly clutching her throat. The shock of the discharge had made her forget her earlier intent to stop McGillie using the weapon against Barney.

She knew before the other outlaws that the discharged bullet had hit the small Frenchman. He was blinking again in that same hypnotic fashion. As they all looked on, friend and foe alike, he made a noise not unlike the laughing which had preceded his first appearance.

This time, however, he was not trying to laugh. He was struggling to breathe. Within a minute he had given up the uneven struggle. His legs bent at the knees and he toppled over, rolling into a prone position and becoming still at once.

Nevada, whose head was still spinning following contact with the fireplace, recovered first. McGillie's mouth was opening and shutting like that of a fish, as he stared at the fallen figure.

'Bruce, train that gun on this fair-headed fellow before he gets frisky again. You hear me?'

McGillie murmured with an effort. 'But what about the Corsican?' No one answered. He lined up his gun on Barney who had risen to a crouching position, and asked: 'You want I should shoot him right now?'

Nevada shook his head. 'Ain't no

hurry now. The action is over. No more surprises in store for us. Except about this hombre cracklin' when he rolls about the floor. Either he has a special sort of bullet-proofin' in the back of that vest, or something of greater interest. His fangs are drawn now. Let's see what it is he carries in his clothing. What do you say, huh?'

McGillie, who did not trust himself to speak, ordered Barney by mime to take off his vest. Barney did so with some show of reluctance. In the middle of this performance, Margaret recovered from the near-swoon after the Corsican's sudden death and planted herself rather uncertainly on an upright chair. She was as interested as the outlaws in the cause of the crackling.

Barney was made to sit at the table with his arms extended upon it. The bearded man kept his gun trained upon him while Nevada slit the lining of the vest and extracted the papers from it. He was disappointed at first, because he had hoped to discover currency notes of a large denomination, or possibly a map, the key to hidden treasure.

His discoveries, however, were of some interest. First, he turned up a sheet with small sketches of Mrs Diamond upon it. He chuckled, studied it from all angles and finally slipped it along the table so that his partner could take a look at it. While McGillie and Margaret were staring with unbelieving eyes at the small sketches, Nevada whistled through his teeth over the other two sheets of drawings.

'Well, what do you know! We turn up a likely enemy of the Kid an' us, all unexpected, an' in the back of his clothes he carries drawings of two of our old buddies. What do you know? Rick an' Joe Tyler. I ain't never seen either of them in a photo but these drawings sure do them justice.'

Barney heard what Nevada was saying, but a part of his mind refused to believe that his half-brothers, Joe and Rick, were friends and allies of Kid Diamond and his gang.

15

In spite of the threat of McGillie's gun, Barney was sufficiently disturbed by what Nevada had said to take a chance. He half rose, and pointed a threatening finger at the tall outlaw.

'You're jest sayin' that! Those are my half-brothers, an' I'd gamble you never met them. You met some men like them, that's all. So stop ridin' me, will you? I never did you any harm before today.'

McGillie clicked back the hammer of his gun, and Barney subsided into his seat watched by the terrified young woman who was pale enough to be on the verge of a faint. The bearded man trained his gun on the upper part of Barney's face, but he appeared to relax quite quickly. He was so sure of himself that he holstered his weapon and started to laugh, walking behind the prisoner as he did so.

He said: 'Joe an' Rick Tyler. That sure is a surprise. Here we are in the back of nowhere an' we turn up pictures of two ex-members of the gang. Hidden in the clothing of a young hombre who's actin' hostile. I wonder what this — this half-brother wanted with them?'

Barney clenched his fists, but remained seated when he saw a certain look on Margaret's face. He closed his lips tightly and pinned them that way with his teeth.

A short silence built up, with each person in the room brooding over exciting thoughts. Everyone except the Corsican. Margaret was perplexed over everything. The magnificent sketches of herself, the outlaw's death and the threat to Barney Malone and herself. Almost forgotten for the moment was the fact that Victor Pardoe wanted her back with him.

'They left home in Brazos Springs a few years back. I quit Texas at the same time because I wanted to go with them. But I lost them on the journey an' I haven't seen them since. They're not like you make out at all!'

Some of Barney's distress showed in his voice as he protested. The two outlaws were silent for a minute or more. They were comparing what Barney had said with what they already knew. Nevada was the one to take up the discussion.

'Homely lookin' fellows, the Tyler boys, I always thought. What with their short upper lips an' bony foreheads. Joe, with his long neck and ginger hair was no picture. He surprised me when he grew that beard to cover up the cleft in his chin. He always looked his best, I thought, when he had his mask on.'

For a short time, Nevada and McGillie rocked with laughter. Barney was shaking with anguish, but he kept still for a time, wanting to hear more. He figured there was more to come and that it could not make pleasant hearing. Margaret Diamond appeared to be sharing his misery. Her feelings showed in her face.

McGillie nibbled a finger nail and spat out a sliver, before going on. 'Rick's hair was a better colour. Auburn, would you say? He had that same bony forehead, but he put it to good use. He butted people with it in fights. He had those long ear lobes, too. They sure did used to puff up when he took a punch on them.'

Neither of the outlaws were giving any regard to the drawings. They were talking from personal knowledge. At the same time, they were deliberately playing upon Barney's emotions. He reacted rather more swiftly than they anticipated, lunging backwards in his chair and catching the stiffly built bearded character with a swinging right hander about belt level.

McGillie meant to step backwards, but the force of the blow made his progress a stagger. For nearly a minute the two of them rolled on the floor, wrestling furiously. It might have gone on for much longer if Nevada had not knocked over the table and hurled himself across to take a hand. Margaret thought Barney's time was running out as the tall man drew a revolver, and stood over the wrestlers.

She screamed, and Barney jerked his head as the butt of the gun was aimed at his temple. The blow landed further back than Nevada had intended and merely scraped the skin. The sight of Nevada baring his teeth and hesitating as to whether he should strike a blow or fire a shot had the effect of terminating Barney's efforts. He rolled aside, stood up and raised his hands.

He thought he probably looked a rather forlorn figure, but at that time he did not care very much what sort of an impression he gave. Margaret, for her part, was relieved that he had taken the discreet way out. She did not want another killing in her house, particularly if it involved the death of a friendly person.

McGillie brutally struck Barney several times in the chest and abdomen while Nevada kept the gun handy, but eventually the two outlaws were content to truss their victim and put off any further decision about him until later.

Presently, Margaret was able to coax her unwanted guests to eat. They finished the first pan full of bacon before doing any more talking. It was when the next round was being transferred to their plates that Nevada began to feel really mean again. He turned to where Barney was lying and pointed at him.

'If it's of any interest to you, brother, those boys you were on about are no use to you. Joe's been dead this twelve month, an' Rick is in jail. Rick's lungs are so bad he ain't expected to live out his sentence.'

Barney, lying with the whipcord cutting into his limbs, felt so low that this devastating piece of information had no immediate effect upon him.

★ ★ ★

When Dan Moore left Ford that morning, he felt reasonably sure that he ought to be turning his attention to the remote house where Margaret Diamond was supposed to be. He was so concerned about the Kid, however, and the wanton damage which he might commit as he moved away from town, that he detoured on no less than three occasions to check that people living in isolated places had not been visited by the killer.

Each time he called, he was well received, but his vigilance made him later and later as he proceeded towards the Diamonds' out of town house. His last detour had thrown him off the route outlined in town, and consequently, he had to use his knowledge of the country to get back on his course.

The watercourse seemed to be his best guide and he followed it, although it added quite considerably to the distance he had to travel. He was still unaware of the closeness of the cabin until he located Margaret's bathing spot where the stream widened.

The wooden bridge attracted his

attention first, and then he discovered a muddied patch where the hooves of horses had cut up the bank. That was enough to give him the direction of the house. Next, he headed away from the water over rising terrain. Topping a rise, he pulled up abruptly, surprised and very much on the alert from what he could see.

Beyond the trees in which he was half hidden, at a distance of perhaps five or six hundred yards, he identified the house amid more trees. He was in his most cautious mood when he dismounted and slid his Winchester from its place in the saddle scabbard.

The dun snorted and shook itself, while he walked forward and studied the setting of the house from behind the bole of a large oak on the very edge of the timber stand. He went back and fetched his spyglass as a figure emerged from the house, dragging a burden which trailed along the ground.

The glass made things adequately clear. The man who had dragged out the burden was stripped to the waist. He was Barney Malone, and when the burden was out of his hands he started to dig with a short-handled shovel.

A tall man in dark riding gear came out of the cabin and studied the digger with his hands hooked to his gun belt by the thumbs. Barney looked up at the other, but he applied himself to the digging. Dan was interested to see that Barney was working on a grave. Moreover, he had a body with which to fill it.

Outlaws. These men who had the drop on Barney must be outlaws. It needed no stretch of imagination to figure them for members of the Kid's gang. And, judging by what Dan could see, the corpse was likely to be another member of the renegade outfit. That meant, probably, that Barney had been in action; that he had eliminated one of them. Dan thought about the situation while he watched another man, one with a rounded fair beard, come out into the open and casually take in the digging situation while he smoked what looked like a short cigar.

Two outlaws, at least. Nevada wandered away through the trees. As he moved from one shadowy spot to another, it was clear to Dan who had clashed with them before whose features he was seeing. He liked to think that the dead one was the Corsican. The little dark man had a habit of popping up just when he was least expected. He had in the past put Dan's nerves on edge.

Nevada and McGillie were just as deadly, but perhaps they were more predictable. Dan witnessed the quiet hostility of McGillie for the woman when she came out of the house and insisted upon giving Barney a mug of liquid to quench his thirst.

Dan then had confirmation of Margaret's being there. He thought that if she had been anywhere else at all in the world at this critical time his task might be that much easier. The worried deputy sighed. He had a feeling in the back of his mind that the outlaws might already have decided Barney's fate, in which case, he — Dan — would have to make some sort of a one-man attack upon the killers in an effort to preserve the artist's life.

What Dan was anticipating was that Barney might be shot when he had finished digging the grave; that he might then have to share it with the other corpse. Such a course of action, however, was not in the minds of the renegades. When the time came to transfer the body to the grave, Barney was given a brief spell off and then forced to throw in the soil on top of the corpse.

Dan found himself breaking out in cold perspiration. He felt a kind of relief, but that was only temporary. Within minutes of Barney having finished his task, a solitary rider started to approach the building from another direction. This rider was on the opposite side from Dan, and coming in at an angle. Something about the way the newcomer sat the saddle gave the watching deputy an inkling as to who he was.

This was the Kid, also arriving late at the Diamond cabin. Dan groaned. He had his shoulder weapon to hand, and yet he knew before he put it to his shoulder that anyone around the building was beyond accurate shooting rage. Kid Diamond was unaware of his presence, but the distance made his chances of survival almost certain.

In that event, Dan watched the top outlaw through his gun sights but made no effort to pull the trigger. He thought that his luck was really out. Here were the key figures in Barney's life and his own, all congregated in a single place, and nothing in the present circumstances could be done about them without endangering the lives of a woman and an innocent young man.

Would the Kid order a couple of executions to make up for his frustration in the old dentist's house in town? Dan truly could not have predicted what would happen when the leader came together with his men and discovered the new circumstances. The elimination of one of his number might be more than sufficient to start the Kid on a killing spree. All Dan could do was hold back and wait.

16

That night was one of the most trying which Dan Moore could ever remember living through. He had to eat a cold supper which did not do him a lot of good, and he had to put down his sleeping roll in a position where he could keep a check on the comings and goings, if any, at the house.

There was not much noise. He heard and saw enough to be certain that the Kid was insisting upon a night watch. Dan, had he been in the other's place, would certainly have taken the same precautions. No one came out from town to represent the law or the Dime saloon, and Dan felt curious about that. He figured after a while that so few people had ever been taken to this remote house that they would not now want to break with tradition.

An hour after sunrise, all was activity

at the house. Men came and went, and Dan could only surmise that the Kid had ordered an evacuation. This was in fact true, and the people who had used the building during that night all emerged and moved towards the riding horses which were given a thorough inspection before they started out.

Margaret Diamond was assisted against her wishes into the saddle of her pinto mare. She was in riding rig, looking very much like a young man. Her sensitive features were hidden from the observer by the shade afforded by her hat brim. McGillie kept close to her in case she decided to make an unpredicted move. Nevada took it upon himself to be the personal guard of Barney, who was mounted up on his own grey stallion.

The Kid forked the palomino on which he had arrived, and he led a spare riding horse which carried some of their gear. This animal was a bay gelding for which the Corsican had no further use. One minute they were all frisking around in the timber and the next they had headed out.

Dan felt frustrated and increasingly anxious. On the face of things, the gang had some specific rendezvous in mind. Either that, or they were taking their two prisoners along as insurance in case they were ambushed by peace officers. Dan was not to find out until later that pressure had been put on Barney and Margaret to reveal the reason why one had visited the other.

Around ten in the morning by riding at a brisk pace, the Kid's party had bypassed Ford and cut across the main trail which connected that township with Redrock Wells further east. No other travellers had been close enough to see them as they crossed the trail and it was not until they were almost a mile beyond the track that the Kid permitted them to ease up.

To Dan, who followed with all the speed he could muster without being observed, the ride was anything but a pleasant one. He had this far no idea of the Kid's plans, and all he knew was that two innocent people were in grave danger if he did anything openly to threaten the gang's progress.

A little after noon, the party slowed and Nevada found for them a small secluded glade in which they could rest for a time unobserved. Dan, in his role of tracker and observer, continued to come up with them and so that he did not have to pull up still in the rear, he manoeuvred himself around the west side of their position.

Fortunately for him, he discovered a thin trickle of fresh water. This sufficed to quench his thirst and that of his mount. He was also able to fill his canteen and eat a few biscuits. Biscuits were becoming his staple diet, and if the situation had not been so tricky he would certainly have taken time out to try and catch some fish or trap a rabbit.

As he could not afford to rest properly, he passed some of his waiting time by grooming his horse. When this was finished, he went on foot a little nearer to the secluded glade. To his surprise he saw his old enemy, Diamond, stride out into the open with his head down and come towards him. Dan had with him his Winchester, and the weight of it, dragging on his arm reminded him of its usefulness.

This time the Kid was much nearer to him. In fact, he was well within range of a bullet from a good marksman. Dan licked his lips. He stepped behind a tree and tried to weigh up the situation. The Kid had a good brain and at this particular time he was seeking to use it. He had walked away from the rest of the party so as not to be distracted.

Dan started to breath shallowly, as though the sound of his breathing could carry to his enemy. The Kid slowed up, half stumbled over a tree root and leaned against the bole of the tree in question. He looked up after a few seconds, but his eyes were not upon anything in particular.

Dan put the Winchester to his shoulder. He did not want to think about this situation. The Kid had tried to kill him only a short while ago. Surely he did not deserve a warning as to what was about to occur. Dan panned the gun a little, lined it up on the Kid's head and pulled the trigger. Had the Kid not been standing sideways a shot at his trunk would have been better. Dan's aim was good, but not good enough. The light grey stetson which the Kid had started wearing since he lost his straw hat left his head and flew off sideways.

The Kid ducked, dropped into the grass and rolled away from the critical position. The bunch grass was long in the area. Neither the hat nor the man who was wriggling away could be detected after that. Cursing quietly to himself, Dan backed away. He had done the unforgiveable. He had drawn a bead on his enemy and missed. How could he have done that? When he calmed down a little he blamed it on the outsize grey hat, but having apportioned the blame he did not feel any better. Now, he had warned his enemies of his presence, and they would be far more on the alert from this time forward.

* * *

When the outlaw party moved off again, Margaret Diamond was sharing the back of the palomino horse with the outlaw boss and Barney and his grey were tightly bunched between Nevada and McGillie. The renegades did not spend any time at all in looking around for the hidden marksman. With two prisoners closely in their midst they knew they were safe.

That night, they camped out in a gully which was easy to defend. Dan, who dared not move in and attack them for obvious reasons, went on ahead and camped some two to three miles further south. By that time, he thought he knew what the Kid's plans were. There was no future in keeping Barney, but Margaret might be a useful source of revenue to men in their unusual position.

They knew by this time that Victor Pardoe had money. With her in their power, they could bargain with the desperate old doctor for her safe return. It was clear to Dan that Pardoe would part with most of his fortune to get Margaret back. His feelings for her had deepened rather than otherwise while she had been away from him. Moreover, the place where the doctor lived was out in the country. His house might make a useful retreat for the gang to hide in.

All this reasoning Dan did on his own around his fire that night. He had taken a risk in lighting one, but it was a calculated risk and he felt that it was worthwhile. The one direction in which his enemies would not expect to find him was ahead of them. They did not come near him, and shortly after dawn, he broke camp, went to some trouble to obliterate his traces and set about putting himself back in touch again.

Conchas Creek and Dr Pardoe's house were too far away at this juncture to gamble that the party was headed there. Dan felt reasonably sure, but he could be wrong, and the Kid might have a change of heart. That being so, Dan had to backtrack a little and start his observation again.

In order to further his observation and to avoid blundering into the larger party, he deliberately rode a little further west than the route they were likely to take and ascended an eroded spur of rock which seemed much higher than he had thought in the early light of morning.

For a time, he had to concentrate upon his climb. He was out of sight of the land lower down, being hidden in a fold of the ascending outcrop. When at last he reached a good vantage point on the east side near the top he found that another development had occurred. The eastern side of the rocky hill presented an aspect like a cliff, and almost underneath it on that side were two or three hollows devoid of grass and sandy in colour.

The Kid had divested himself of the least useful of his prisoners. In the middle of one sandy hollow was a towering needle of rock. A rope had been attached to the needle and to the other end of it was fastened a trussed man; namely, Barney Malone. The young artist had with him his hat, and he was fully dressed, but he had no weapons or anything with which to defend himself in the event of an attack by animals or humans.

Dan whistled to himself. A distant cloud of dust showed where the rest of the party had gone. But Barney was down there and he was in difficulties. What could a man do who ought to be in two places at once? Barney was a good friend to Dan, a man the latter could do to have around for a long time. But if he toiled down to that spot and freed his friend the outlaws and their female prisoner might be gone from his sight forever.

Dan had a difficult decision to make. He decided that Barney would have to take second place. Having made that decision, he then tried hard to devise a scheme to prevent the young artist from dying of thirst. He had to be given the means of freeing himself. A knife was wanted.

The sun was already working its way into that hollow of sand and very soon, Barney, trussed as he was, hand and foot, and only able to move about in a narrow circle, limited by the length of the lariat, would begin to suffer.

Dan had only the one knife. He could not afford to lose it, or to drop it outside the target area which was Barney's hollow. How, then, could he be sure to drop it in the right place? Five minutes of perspiration and troubled thought in the broiling sun produced the answer. The knife had to be attached to something. A larger shaft of some sort. A stick. A tree branch . . .

Dan found such a branch. It was the stem rather than a branch of a young sapling growing out of the side of the cliff with very little soil to support it. While he worked on the wooden shaft, Dan deliberately rolled stones and earth down the side of the cliff. He felt sure that the Kid had not left anyone behind to try and trap him.

Presently, Barney became aware of the trickle. He peered up, careful not to dislodge his hat, and perceived his friend waving from far above him. Dan persevered and presently he had the knife lashed to the end of the sapling like the head of a primitive spear.

He stood up rather carefully. If anything went wrong with his throw he promised himself that he would have to go all the way down to Barney and release him, even though the Kid was getting away with his female prisoner. Even though such a course of action would be against Barney's wishes.

He practised for nearly five minutes and the perspiration was running from his forehead and his shoulders and arms by the time he felt he was ready for the long throw. He was in a state of nerves, but the job had to be done, and without delay. At last he summoned up his courage and made the cast.

Was it off-target? No, *but was it too close to the trussed man?* Eventually, it kicked up dust and sand within twenty feet of the prisoner who acknowledged and started to wriggle towards it.

17

The descent was more difficult than going up. Dan came down mustering all possible speed without sacrificing his safety. His shirt was saturated before he reached the valley floor and by that time the sandy hollows were out of sight and some distance to the rear.

Dan felt that this protracted clash with the Diamond gang might be resolved that very day. In order to have a chance to win it, he had to be ruthless and exercise singleness of purpose. Consequently, he put the trials of his friend, Barney, strictly behind him and did all in his power to get back in touch with the main part.

One or two brief occurrences warned him whereabouts they might be, and once he was sure he detoured again and went around them, determined to arrive at Pardoe's place ahead of them so that some sort of action could be mounted for when they arrived.

The journey took him longer than he had expected. The evening was well advanced when he jogged down the last slope north of the retired doctor's house and entered in upon the flat patch of ground which was cultivated.

Gardens had been laid out on both sides of the one-storey house and stable, but since Margaret had gone away, Pardoe had dispensed with his gardener and allowed the growing plots to run wild. Dan sent his dun up a path between two of them and raised his damp hat as Pardoe himself appeared at the rear door of the building.

The older man's face looked anything but happy as he stood under the wooden arch outside the door with flowers of every hue above and beside him. Clearly, Pardoe had hoped to see Barney rather than Dan, but any friendly face to a lonely person is better than none at all. Dan flopped to the ground and allowed his surprised host to take charge of his mount.

Five minutes of staccato talk on Dan's part was sufficient to make Pardoe understand what had been happening and what was still to come. Dan did not sound at all cheerful as he weighed the possibilities of what might happen in the near future.

One thing was clear. Pardoe was prepared to do all in his power to safeguard Margaret's future, and that went for Dan, too. The ex-doctor was prepared to kill, if need be, and he said as much.

'How much time do we have?' he asked, as the discussion came to an end.

'Unfortunately, I can't say. It might be hours, after dark, an' then again it might happen very shortly. We have to do all we can to be ready. That's all I can say.'

Pardoe summed up the situation. He came around the building while Dan was busy at the pump carrying a ladder. Presently, he was at the top of the ladder propped against a tree on the north side of the tiny estate. While he was up there keeping watch through a glass, further discussion went on.

Having cleaned himself, Dan partook of cold rabbit pie and followed that up with fruit. Next, he went to work on his weapons, giving them the first good clean for days. After that, the deputy had to find a hiding place from which he could give the outlaws the maximum of surprise.

'Try the well,' Pardoe suggested. 'This is the only house I know of near here which has both a well and a pump.'

Dan moved towards the well which was in the centre of a small cleared space directly behind the house. He had no great confidence in the well as a place to hole up, but a brief examination showed him its possibilities. Some four feet below the top the builder had contrived a stone ledge which ran all the way round, inside, a foot in width.

It was a little narrow for a man to

crouch on, but a wooden plank was across
the well, spanning the ledge from one
side to the other. Dan vaulted into the
top and knelt. He then eased up a little
and took a careful look around. His eyes
were bright when he vaulted out again
and collected his weapons. Somehow,
he had had his confidence restored.

The clash which lay ahead of them
could not fail to end in bloodshed. For
the first time that day, Dan felt quietly
confident. Within minutes Pardoe
called a warning from the top of his
ladder. He came down quite quickly,
intimating that he had made his first
sighting of the party.

Dan at once tensed up, but he
marvelled as the older man hauled the
ladder away and at the same time
dragged his coat to cover up the horse
tracks made earlier. Pardoe was thorough. The tired dun was already in the
stable. If its presence was queried
before the surprise was sprung, the
ex-doctor was prepared to lie his way
out of trouble.

One minute the isolated home was all quiet and the next minute horses were moving into it. Nevada and McGillie came up the garden riding side by side. One of them was on the intended path and the other on the neglected garden. Both were strictly on the alert for surprises.

They studied the layout of the house and its rear, nodded to one another and neatly dismounted, pushing their horses aside and still keeping up a sharp watch. The well head was stared at by each man, but nothing about it occasioned any suspicion. The outlaws murmured together. They parted company, moved around the exterior of the house to the other side and came back again.

All that could be heard from the interior was a faint sound of music. Pardoe was playing his upright piano. Nevada sniffed and thumped on the back door with the butt of his rifle.

McGillie stepped back a pace or two and blew his nose in the dust. The sound of the piano stopped and Nevada also backed off a few paces, bringing up his gun barrel.

Before Pardoe could answer the door, the Kid and Margaret came down the path on the back of Barney's dappled grey horse. Behind them, they had the Kid's palomino. Its back was drooping through having carried a double load. There was no sign of the other horse. It had been turned loose, having suffered a slight sprain.

Hatless and watchful, Dan took in everything from inside the well. The next move was up to Pardoe, but he was a long time in coming. The Kid lowered Margaret rather roughly to the ground. He slipped down beside her, relying upon his .44s to offset any sort of surprise.

The grey moved wearily towards the left of the house, the direction of the stable. Margaret gravitated a few feet that way herself, and so did the Kid who was watching the door rather than the woman. Suddenly it opened and Dr Pardoe was there in a loose-fitting coat, a tiny skull cap and slippers. A pair of clip-on spectacles hid the brightness of his brown eyes.

He nodded to his wife, dragged his eyes away from her, and mustered what dignity he could for the benefit of the men. 'Gents, I can't say you're welcome here, although you have brought my wife along. I have to tell you that hostile guns are trained on you at this very moment.'

Pardoe coughed. Margaret gasped. The three marauders sprang about. Only the horses moved as if nothing was at stake. Pardoe was left there framed in his floral arch, apparently regarded by all as a mere pawn in what was to follow.

Dan brought up the barrel of his Winchester and shot Nevada expertly through the head. He moved his gun in the direction of the Kid for his second target because Diamond had lunged towards Margaret again thinking to use her as a shield. A moving horse baulked Dan, and laid him open to retaliatory fire from McGillie, who — as always — was reasonably accurate. One bullet hit the bucket, swinging above Dan's head and another tweaked the bandanna, loosely tied at his throat.

The deputy moved again, caught a glimpse of McGillie beyond the horse and at once blasted him. Hit in the shoulder, the bearded man pivoted on his heels, dropped to the ground and rolled away. His guns were silent for a while. Meantime, Margaret, who had had more than enough of Diamond's close attentions on the ride, acted out of character. She kicked the kid in a vital spot as he was aiming his weapon at Dan.

Pain interfered with his further efforts. Blinking hard to clear his vision, the Kid swayed and rocked, and fired off his gun haphazardly, his intention being to bring down both Dan and the woman. Bullets chipped the sides of the well head; Margaret was knocked sideways. At the critical climax of the shooting match, Pardoe pulled a revolver from the foliage beside him and managed to shoot the Kid low in the stomach. Dan vaulted into view, and removed all weapons from Diamond and Nevada. He had an inkling that McGillie was not dead, and he managed to finish off the wounded man with a telling shot just as the latter lined up on him.

Pardoe had discarded his weapon and he was beside Margaret who had flopped to the ground when Dan got around to sizing up the situation. The Kid's wild shooting had put a bullet high in her right shoulder. Between them they carried her indoors and laid her on a bed which she had once shared. While Pardoe got out his hold-all and prepared to remove the bullet, Dan came out again.

He was in time to see Barney arrive on the back of the bay gelding which had once carried Ludeau. He had forced it to get him here, although its sprain had been badly aggravated. Barney at once put his knife to the throat of Kid Diamond whose time was obviously running out. He learned what he most wanted to know, although the knowledge hurt him.

His half-brothers, Joe and Rick, had never really been away in the army as his parents had led him to believe. They had been in jail. When he had followed them away from home that time, Rick had deliberately knocked him off the observation platform of the train. Later, Diamond explained, they had held up the express car. In getting rid of him, they had done him a favour.

Barney groaned. He straightened up and allowed his friend to lead him indoors. They were in time to see the doctor take out the Kid's bullet from Margaret's shoulder. She was only semi-conscious, but Pardoe thanked the two young men for both of them.

A short while later, they were walking in the garden on the other side of the house when Dan remembered the Kid.

They turned with one accord and went to look him over. Barney was the one to produce a canteen, but Diamond died before he could drink. He died with his vicious eyes drained of their accustomed venom, but that split eyelid still made Dan shudder as it closed for the last time.

While Margaret slept, the three men dined together. Vic produced cigars for his friends and appeared to be the most light-hearted of them all.

'You're wondering about the future, I don't doubt. By the time Margaret's wound is mended I shall have persuaded her that she should be back here under my care and protection. She's got pride and she won't want to stay, but I won her affection once before an' I think she'll listen to me again.'

'I think she'll stay, Doc,' Dan opined. 'I'm goin' to try an' persuade old Marshman to retire. If he does, I'll be after his job. Barney doesn't know it yet, but I'll be wantin' him for my deputy for a while because Jabez' protege hasn't got what it takes.'

Pardoe and Dan both stared at the fair young man. He had taken grave risks and done them both a lot of good. The doctor said: 'I owe you money, Barney, and I can give you more artistic work, if you want it.'

Barney, who had just realized that his self-imposed wanderings were over, yawned, grinned and spread his hands. 'Okay, okay, I'll stay. It wouldn't surprise me if I had to draw some weddin' pictures real soon.'

Dan, who was abreast of his friend's thinking, blushed under his tan.

THE END